²² But the fruit of the Spirit is love, joy, peace, forbearance, kindness, goodness, faithfulness, ²³ gentleness and self-control. Against such things there is no law.

(Galatians; Chapter 5, Verse 22-23)

²² 聖靈所結的果子,就是仁愛、喜樂、和平、忍耐、恩慈、良善、信實、²³ 溫柔、節制。這樣的事沒有律法禁止。

(加拉太書;5章,22-23節)

全音檔下載導向頁面

https://globalv.com.tw/mp3-download-9789864544158/

掃描 QR 碼進入網頁並註冊後,按「全書音檔下載請按此」連結,可一次性下載音檔壓縮檔,或點選檔名線上播放。
全 MP3 一次下載為 ZIP 壓縮檔,部分智慧型手機需安裝解壓縮程式方可開啟,iOS 系統請升級至 iOS 13 以上。
此為大型檔案,建議使用 WIFI 連線下載,以免占用流量,並請確認連線狀況,以利下載順暢。

閱讀最激勵人心的聖經金句，從抄寫中培養 9 種人性美德！

以聖經中加拉太書五章 22、23 節「仁愛、喜樂、和平、忍耐、恩慈、良善、信實、溫柔、節制」的九種美德貫穿全書。透過激勵靈性的聖句，讓讀者在一邊閱讀、一邊抄寫的同時，再搭配聆聽與跟讀，來反覆鍛鍊自我的心性及英文能力。

✎ 精心摘錄的經句抄寫書

9 大主題、9 種美德，135 天超過一季的內容設計，以最廣泛的中英文聖經版本為基準：英文以新國際版（New International Version），中文以和合本，來作為互相的對照。

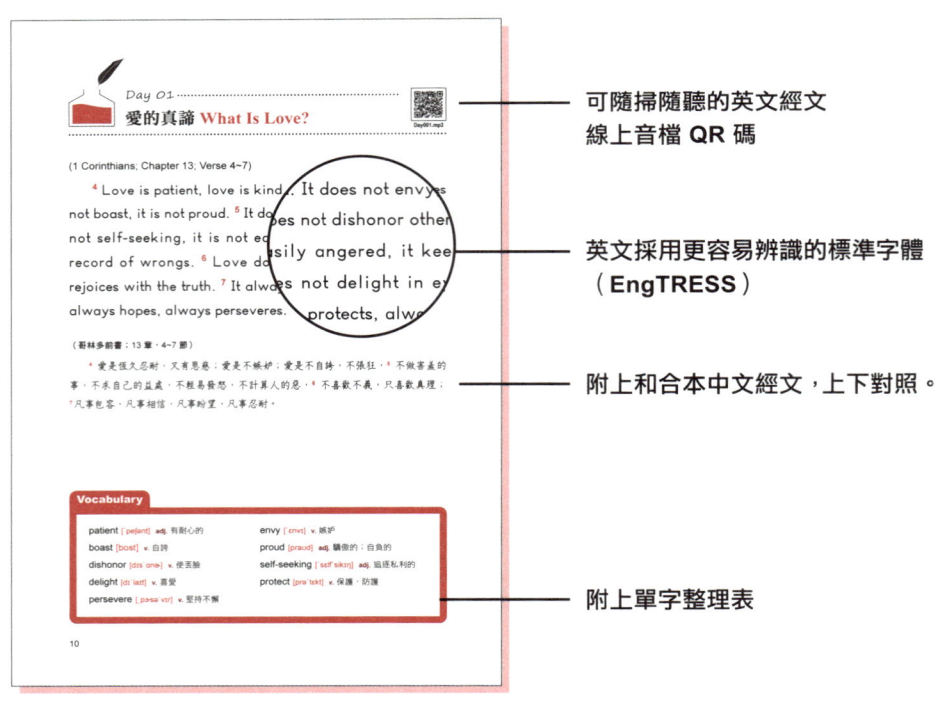

✎ 標準4線英文書寫格的抄寫頁面

如同英語作業簿的4條直線英文書寫格,本書的抄寫書寫格讓讀者的英文抄寫更加整齊、乾淨,對齊時也不會眼花撩亂。

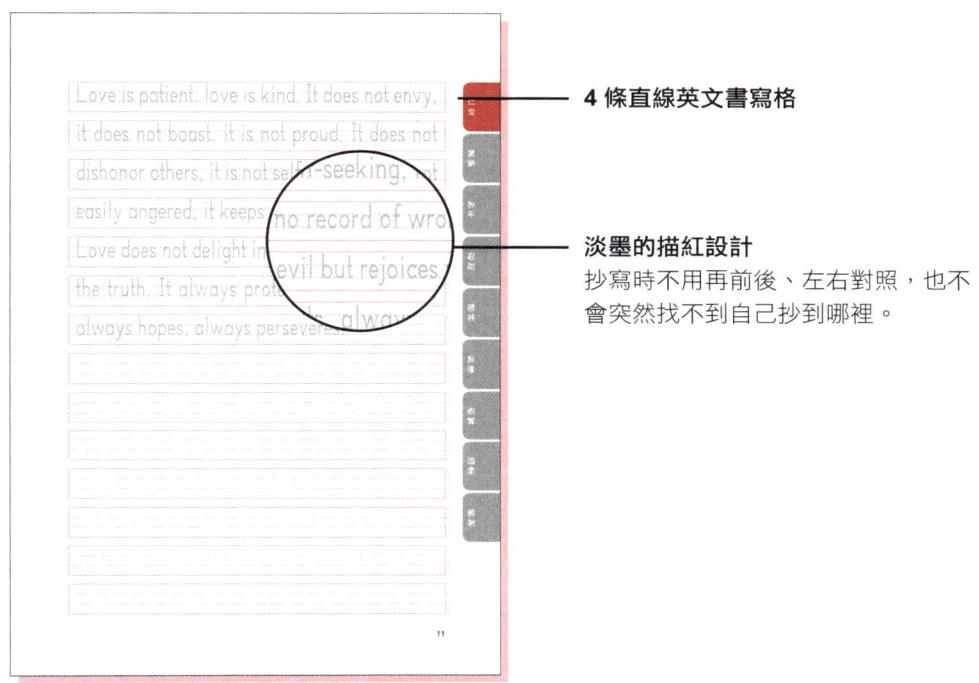

4條直線英文書寫格

淡墨的描紅設計
抄寫時不用再前後、左右對照,也不會突然找不到自己抄到哪裡。

✎ 2 種版本的經句朗讀音檔

除了每一天隨掃隨聽的線上音檔,本書在第 1 頁還提供全書下載的 QR 碼,並分成 2 種版本的英文經文音檔。一為純人聲版本的朗讀音檔;一為有襯樂版本的朗讀音檔。

・**純人聲版本**:檔名為「Sound Only」的資料夾
・**有襯樂版本**:檔名為「With Music」的資料夾

目錄

Chapter 1 仁愛 LOVE ········ 9

- **Day 01** 愛的真諦 What Is Love? ········ 10
- **Day 02** 天父的愛 Love from God ········ 12
- **Day 03** 神愛世人 God Loves the World ········ 14
- **Day 04** 基督的愛 Christ's Love ········ 16
- **Day 05** 豐盛的愛 Great Love ········ 18
- **Day 06** 平安的愛 Love in Peace ········ 20
- **Day 07** 誡命與愛 Commands and Love ········ 22
- **Day 08** 愛不虛假 Love without Affectation ········ 24
- **Day 09** 愛無懼怕 Love without Fear ········ 26
- **Day 10** 愛的全德 Love in Perfect Unity ········ 28
- **Day 11** 愛的照顧 Care the Least Ones ········ 30
- **Day 12** 愛的激勵 Love Compels Us ········ 32
- **Day 13** 愛的犧牲 Love's Sacrifice ········ 34
- **Day 14** 愛你仇敵 Love Your Enemies ········ 36
- **Day 15** 博愛大眾 Love Everyone ········ 38

Chapter 2 喜樂 JOY ········ 41

- **Day 16** 靠主得喜樂 Rejoice in the LORD ········ 42
- **Day 17** 喜樂的來源 The Source of Joy ········ 44
- **Day 18** 大大的喜樂 Rejoiced Greatly in the LORD ········ 46
- **Day 19** 不憂慮之樂 Do Not Worry ········ 48
- **Day 20** 滿足的喜樂 Fill with Joy ········ 50
- **Day 21** 患難中喜樂 Glory in Sufferings ········ 52
- **Day 22** 試煉中喜樂 Face Trials with Joy ········ 54
- **Day 23** 喜樂的生活 Rejoice Always ········ 56
- **Day 24** 喜樂的同伴 Rejoice with Those Who Rejoice ········ 58
- **Day 25** 喜樂的歡呼 Shouts of Joy ········ 60
- **Day 26** 喜樂與平安 Joy and Peace ········ 62
- **Day 27** 喜樂與思想 Be Happy and Be Thoughtful ········ 64
- **Day 28** 喜樂與盼望 Joy and Hope ········ 66
- **Day 29** 喜樂為良藥 Cheerful Heart Is Good Medicine ········ 68
- **Day 30** 喜樂過生活 Live in Joy ········ 70

Chapter 3 和平 PEACE ········ 73

- **Day 31** 神國在乎和平 God's Kingdom Is a Matter of Peace ········ 74
- **Day 32** 和平從上頭來 Peace from Heaven ········ 76

Day 33	和平的君降生 Prince of Peace Is Given 78
Day 34	傳揚和平福音 Come and Preach Peace 80
Day 35	同心追求和平 Pursue Peace 82
Day 36	不與他人相爭 Don't Accuse Others 84
Day 37	追求與人和睦 Live in Peace with Everyone 86
Day 38	彼此不發怨言 Without Grumbling or Arguing 88
Day 39	務要彼此和睦 Live in Peace with Each Other 90
Day 40	不與弟兄動怒 Don't Be Angry with Others 92
Day 41	無限饒恕弟兄 Forgive Seventy-seven Times 94
Day 42	弟兄和睦同居 Live Together in Unity 96
Day 43	不要以惡報惡 Don't Repay Evil with Evil 98
Day 44	善待你的仇敵 Be Kind to Your Enemy 100
Day 45	與仇敵和好 Make Peace with Enemies 102

Chapter 4 忍耐 FORBEARANCE 105

Day 46	效法耶穌忍耐 Learn from Jesus's Endurance 106
Day 47	忍耐行神旨意 Persevere till God's Will Is Done 108
Day 48	忍耐不覺受苦 Glory Overcomes Present Sufferings 110

Day 49	忍耐受苦榜樣 Example of Patience 112
Day 50	忍耐以致結實 By Persevering Produce a Crop 114
Day 51	忍耐必得開路 The Way to Endurance 116
Day 52	忍耐必蒙記念 Endurance Will Be Remembered 118
Day 53	忍耐免去試煉 Endurance Keeps from the Trial 120
Day 54	忍耐受迫得福 Blessed Are Those Who Are Persecuted 122
Day 55	行善受苦忍耐 Suffer for Doing Good 124
Day 56	患難中要忍耐 Patient in Affliction 126
Day 57	歡歡喜喜忍耐 Endurance and Patience with Joy 128
Day 58	忍耐恩典夠用 Grace Is Sufficient 130
Day 59	忍耐望見未來 Endurance Achieves Eternal Glory 132
Day 60	忍耐直到主來 Be Patient until the LORD's Coming 134

Chapter 5 恩慈 KINDNESS 137

Day 61	神以恩慈救人 Saved by God's Grace 138
Day 62	神的恩慈顯明 God's Kindness Appears 140
Day 63	神的恩慈憐憫 God's Mercy and Compassion 142
Day 64	神的恩慈照顧 No One Is Cast off by the LORD 144

Day 65	神的恩慈堅定 God's Unfailing Love ········ 146
Day 66	神的恩慈要求 The Mercy God Requires ········ 148
Day 67	選民恩慈存心 The Kindness of God's Chosen Ones ········ 150
Day 68	要以恩慈相待 Be Kind to One Another ········ 152
Day 69	正直人有恩慈 Upright People are Gracious ········ 154
Day 70	恩慈必得豐裕 Generous Person Will Prosper ········ 156
Day 71	恩慈多行善事 Generous on Every Occasion ········ 158
Day 72	恩慈牧養群羊 Care God's Flock with Willing ········ 160
Day 73	恩慈絕不被棄 Never the Righteous Be Forsaken ········ 162
Day 74	恩慈適應眾人 Share Blessings with Everyone ········ 164
Day 75	恩慈嚴厲有別 God's Kindness and Sternness ········ 166

Chapter 6 良善 GOODNESS ········ 169

Day 76	耶和華本為善 The LORD Is Good ········ 170
Day 77	察驗神的善良 Test and Approve God's Will ········ 172
Day 78	聖潔以備行善 Cleanse Ourselves for Doing Good Work ········ 174
Day 79	聖經教導行善 Bible Teaches Good Work ········ 176
Day 80	不可以惡報惡 Nobody Pays Back Wrong for Wrong ········ 178
Day 81	不可忘記行善 Don't Forget to Do Good ········ 180
Day 82	行善不可推辭 Don't Withhold from Doing Good ········ 182
Day 83	行善不可喪志 Don't Become Weary in Doing Good ········ 184
Day 84	行善不求回報 Do Good without Expecting Repayment ········ 186
Day 85	行善如神有光 Shine Your Light on People in Need ········ 188
Day 86	行善就要大方 Be Generous When Doing Good ········ 190
Day 87	求善者得恩惠 Whoever Seeks Good Finds Favor ········ 192
Day 88	依善行得賞賜 Get Rewards for Good Deeds ········ 194
Day 89	持守善美的事 Hold on to What Is Good ········ 196
Day 90	富人更該行善 Rich People Should Do Good Deeds ········ 198

Chapter 7 信實 FAITHFULNESS ········ 201

Day 91	信實神施慈愛 Faithful God Keeping His Covenant of Love ········ 202
Day 92	信實的神可信 God Remains Faithful ········ 204

Day 93	神的應許信實 God's Promise Is Faithful ·········· 206
Day 94	與信實神有分 Faithful God Calls You into Fellowship ·········· 208
Day 95	信實直到萬代 Faithfulness through All Generations ·········· 210
Day 96	信實堅立於天 Faithfulness Is Established in Heaven ·········· 212
Day 97	信實為神所悅 God Delights Trustworthy People ··· 214
Day 98	信實脫離惡者 Faithfulness Protects You from the Evil One ·········· 216
Day 99	信實無可指摘 Become Blameless and Pure ·········· 218
Day 100	信實認真傳道 God's Message Is "Yes" ·········· 220
Day 101	愛心說誠實話 Speaking the Truth in Love ·········· 222
Day 102	與鄰信實相交 Speak the Truth to Each Other ·········· 224
Day 103	說話是非分明 Say Simply 'Yes' or 'No' ·········· 226
Day 104	不可假冒為善 Don't Be Hypocrites ·········· 228
Day 105	向信實神認罪 Confess Our Sins ·········· 230

Chapter 8 溫柔 GENTLENESS ······ 233

Day 106	溫柔的人承受地土 The Meek Inherit the Earth ·········· 234
Day 107	效主溫柔得享安息 Learn from God's Gentleness ·········· 236
Day 108	保羅傳道溫柔勸戒 Paul's Preach Is Gentle ·········· 238
Day 109	內心溫柔極其寶貴 Gentle Inner Is Great in God's Sight ·········· 240
Day 110	性情溫良是有聰明 Even-tempered One Has Understanding ·········· 242
Day 111	快聽慢說慢慢動怒 Quick to Listen, Slow to Speak and Slow to Become Angry ·········· 244
Day 112	尊主為聖溫柔回答 Revere the LORD and Answer Gently ·········· 246
Day 113	溫良的舌是生命樹 Soothing Tongue Is a Tree of Life ·········· 248
Day 114	溫柔回答使怒消退 Gentle Answer Turns Away Wrath ·········· 250
Day 115	智慧溫柔顯出善行 Show Good Deeds in Wisdom and Humility ·········· 252
Day 116	溫柔忍耐愛心寬容 Bear Others in Gentle Love ·········· 254
Day 117	溫和待人善於教導 Kind to Everyone, Able to Teach ···· 256
Day 118	溫柔持家兒女順服 Not Violent but Gentle in Managing the Family ·········· 258
Day 119	存心溫柔照顧信徒 Care for Believers Like a Nursing Mother ·········· 260
Day 120	用溫柔心挽回信徒 Restore Believers Gently ·········· 262

Chapter 9 節制 SELF-CONTROL ······ 265

Day 121 保守你心勝過一切
Above All Else, Guard Your Heart ···· 266

Day 122 約束己心謹慎自守
Be Alert and Fully Sober with
Minds ·· 268

Day 123 制伏己心形同固牆
Lacking Self-control Is Like
a City with Broken Walls ················ 270

Day 124 攻克己身叫身服我
Discipline the Body and
Bring It into Subjection ················ 272

Day 125 世間享受都是虛空
Worldly Pleasures Are
Meaningless ···································· 274

Day 126 有衣有食就當知足
Be Content with Having Food
and Clothing ···································· 276

Day 127 不看自己過於當看
Don't Think of Yourself More
Highly Than You Ought ················ 278

Day 128 不易發怒勝過勇士
Better a Patient Person
Than a Warrior ································ 280

Day 129 節制貪念沒有愁苦
Love of Money Is a Root of Evil ······ 282

Day 130 有了知識要加節制
Add Self-control to Your
Knowledge ······································ 284

Day 131 享受美食也要節制
Enjoy Delicious Food in
Moderation ······································ 286

Day 132 凡事作為不受轄制
Don't Be Mastered by Anything ······ 288

Day 133 謹言慎行以免犯罪
Watch My Ways and Keep
My Tongue from Sin ······················ 290

Day 134 為神管家凡事節制
Be Self-controlled as an
Overseer of God's Household ········ 292

Day 135 勸老年人要有節制
Teach the Older Men to Be
Self-controlled ································ 294

Chapter 1
仁愛

(Proverbs; Chapter 17: Verse 17)

17 A friend loves at all times,
and a brother is born for a time of adversity.

（箴言；17章，17節）

17 朋友乃時常親愛，弟兄為患難而生。

Chapter1.mp3

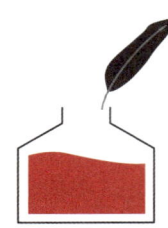

Day 01
愛的真諦 What Is Love?

Day001.mp3

(1 Corinthians; Chapter 13; Verse 4~7)

⁴ Love is patient, love is kind. It does not envy, it does not boast, it is not proud. ⁵ It does not dishonor others, it is not self-seeking, it is not easily angered, it keeps no record of wrongs. ⁶ Love does not delight in evil but rejoices with the truth. ⁷ It always protects, always trusts, always hopes, always perseveres.

（哥林多前書；13 章，4~7 節）

⁴ 愛是恆久忍耐，又有恩慈；愛是不嫉妒；愛是不自誇，不張狂，⁵ 不做害羞的事，不求自己的益處，不輕易發怒，不計算人的惡，⁶ 不喜歡不義，只喜歡真理；⁷ 凡事包容，凡事相信，凡事盼望，凡事忍耐。

Vocabulary

patient [`peʃənt] adj. 有耐心的
boast [bost] v. 自誇
dishonor [dɪs`ɑnɚ] v. 使丟臉
delight [dɪ`laɪt] v. 喜愛
persevere [ˌpɝsə`vɪr] v. 堅持不懈

envy [`ɛnvɪ] v. 嫉妒
proud [praʊd] adj. 驕傲的；自負的
self-seeking [`sɛlf`sikɪŋ] adj. 追逐私利的
protect [prə`tɛkt] v. 保護，防護

Love is patient, love is kind. It does not envy, it does not boast, it is not proud. It does not dishonor others, it is not self-seeking, it is not easily angered, it keeps no record of wrongs. Love does not delight in evil but rejoices with the truth. It always protects, always trusts, always hopes, always perseveres.

仁愛 喜樂 和平 忍耐 恩慈 良善 信實 溫柔 節制

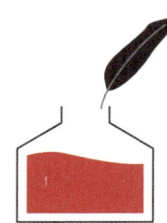

Day 02
天父的愛 Love from God

Day002.mp3

(1 John; Chapter 4: Verse 14-16)

¹⁴ And we have seen and testify that the Father has sent his Son to be the Savior of the world. ¹⁵ If anyone acknowledges that Jesus is the Son of God, God lives in them and they in God. ¹⁶ And so we know and rely on the love God has for us. God is love. Whoever lives in love lives in God, and God in them.

（約翰一書；4 章，14-16 節）

¹⁴ 父差子作世人的救主；這是我們所看見且作見證的。¹⁵ 凡認耶穌為神兒子的，神就住在他裡面，他也住在神裡面。¹⁶ 神愛我們的心，我們也知道也信。神就是愛；住在愛裡面的，就是住在神裡面，神也住在他裡面。

Vocabulary

testify [ˈtɛstəˌfaɪ] v. 作證

acknowledge [əkˈnɑlɪdʒ] v. 承認

rely on v. 依賴

send [sɛnd] v. 送出

live [lɪv] v. 住

whoever [huˈɛvɚ] conj. 無論是誰

And we have seen and testify that the Father has sent his Son to be the Savior of the world. If anyone acknowledges that Jesus is the Son of God, God lives in them and they in God. And so we know and rely on the love God has for us. God is love. Whoever lives in love lives in God, and God in them.

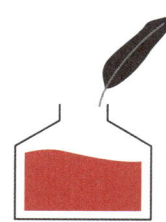

Day 03
神愛世人 God Loves the World

Day003.mp3

(John; Chapter 3: Verse 16-17)

¹⁶ For God so loved the world that he gave his one and only Son, that whoever believes in him shall not perish but have eternal life. ¹⁷ For God did not send his Son into the world to condemn the world, but to save the world through him.

（約翰福音；3章，16-17節）

¹⁶ 神愛世人，甚至將祂的獨生子賜給他們，叫一切信祂的，不致滅亡，反得永生。¹⁷ 因為神差祂的兒子降世，不是要定世人的罪（或作：審判世人；下同），乃是要叫世人因祂得救。

Vocabulary

love [lʌv] v. 愛
give [gɪv] v. 給
eternal [ɪˈtɜːrnəl] adj. 永恆的
save [sev] v. 拯救

world [wɜːrld] n. 世界
believe [bɪˈliːv] v. 相信
condemn [kənˈdɛm] v. 譴責
through [θruː] prep. 透過

For God so loved the world that he gave his one and only Son, that whoever believes in him shall not perish but have eternal life. For God did not send his Son into the world to condemn the world, but to save the world through him.

Day 04
基督的愛 Christ's Love

Day004.mp3

(Romans; Chapter 5: Verse 6-8)

⁶ You see, at just the right time, when we were still powerless, Christ died for the ungodly. ⁷ Very rarely will anyone die for a righteous person, though for a good person someone might possibly dare to die. ⁸ But God demonstrates his own love for us in this: While we were still sinners, Christ died for us.

（羅馬書；5章，6-8節）

⁶ 因我們還軟弱的時候，基督就按所定的日期為罪人死。⁷ 為義人死，是少有的；為仁人死、或者有敢做的。⁸ 惟有基督在我們還作罪人的時候為我們死，神的愛就在此向我們顯明了。

Vocabulary

powerless [ˈpaʊɚləs] adj. 無能的
rarely [ˈrɛrli] adv. 很少
though [ðo] conj. 雖然
dare [dɛr] v. 敢
sinner [ˈsɪnɚ] n. 罪人

ungodly [ˌʌnˈgɒdli] adj. 不敬神的
righteous [ˈraɪtʃəs] adj. 公義的
possibly [ˈpɑːsəbli] adv. 可能
demonstrate [ˈdɛmənˌstret] v. 展示

You see, at just the right time, when we were still powerless, Christ died for the ungodly. Very rarely will anyone die for a righteous person, though for a good person someone might possibly dare to die. But God demonstrates his own love for us in this: While we were still sinners, Christ died for us.

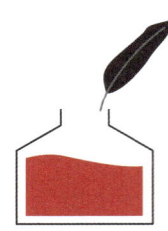

Day 05
豐盛的愛 Great Love

Day005.mp3

(Numbers; Chapter 14: Verse 18-19)

¹⁸ 'The Lord is slow to anger, abounding in love and forgiving sin and rebellion. Yet he does not leave the guilty unpunished; he punishes the children for the sin of the parents to the third and fourth generation.' ¹⁹ In accordance with your great love, forgive the sin of these people, just as you have pardoned them from the time they left Egypt until now."

（民數記；14 章，18-19 節）

¹⁸ 耶和華不輕易發怒，並有豐盛的慈愛，赦免罪孽和過犯；萬不以有罪的為無罪，必追討他的罪，自父及子，直到三、四代。¹⁹ 求祢照祢的大慈愛赦免這百姓的罪孽，好像祢從埃及到如今常赦免他們一樣。

Vocabulary

slow [sloʊ] **adj.** 緩慢的	anger [ˈæŋɡɚ] **n./v.** 憤怒
abound [əˈbaʊndɪŋ] **v.** 豐富	forgive [fɚˈɡɪvɪŋ] **v.** 寬恕
sin [sɪn] **n.** 罪	rebellion [rɪˈbɛljən] **n.** 叛逆
guilty [ˈɡɪlti] **adj.** 有罪的	unpunished [ʌnˈpʌnɪʃt] **adj.** 未受懲罰的
in accordance with 根據	pardon [ˈpardən] **v.** 原諒

18

'The Lord is slow to anger, abounding in love and forgiving sin and rebellion. Yet he does not leave the guilty unpunished; he punishes the children for the sin of the parents to the third and fourth generation.' In accordance with your great love, forgive the sin of these people, just as you have pardoned them from the time they left Egypt until now."

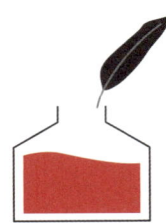

Day 06
平安的愛 Love in Peace

Day006.mp3

(Proverbs; Chapter 15: Verse 16-17)

¹⁶ Better a little with the fear of the Lord than great wealth with turmoil. ¹⁷ Better a small serving of vegetables with love than a fattened calf with hatred.

（箴言；15章，16-17節）

¹⁶ 少有財寶，敬畏耶和華，強如多有財寶，煩亂不安。¹⁷ 吃素菜，彼此相愛，強如吃肥牛，彼此相恨。

Vocabulary

fear [fɪr] **n.** 恐懼
turmoil [ˈtɝ-mɔɪl] **n.** 混亂
fattened [ˈfætn̩d] **adj.** 肥胖的
hatred [ˈheɪtrɪd] **n.** 仇恨

wealth [wɛlθ] **n.** 財富
serving [ˈsɝːvɪŋ] **n.**（供餐）一份，一客
calf [kæf] **n.** 小牛

Better a little with the fear of the Lord than great wealth with turmoil. Better a small serving of vegetables with love than a fattened calf with hatred.

Day 07
誡命與愛 Commands and Love

(Proverbs; Chapter 3: Verse 1-3)

¹ My son, do not forget my teaching, but keep my commands in your heart, ² for they will prolong your life many years and bring you peace and prosperity. ³ Let love and faithfulness never leave you; bind them around your neck, write them on the tablet of your heart.

（箴言；3章，1-3節）

¹ 我兒、不要忘記我的法則〔或作指教〕；你心要謹守我的誡命。² 因為它必將長久的日子、生命的年數、與平安、加給你。³ 不可使慈愛、誠實離開你，要繫在你頸項上，刻在你心版上。

Vocabulary

command [kəˈmænd] n. 誡命；命令
prolong [prəˈlɔŋ] v. 延長
prosperity [prɑˈspɛrɪtɪ] n. 繁榮
bind [baɪnd] v. 綁住，繫
tablet [ˈtæblɪt] n. 牌；塊

for [fɔːr] conj. 因為
peace [piːs] n. 和平
faithfulness [ˈfeθfəlnɪs] n. 忠誠
neck [nɛk] n. 脖子

My son, do not forget my teaching, but keep my commands in your heart, for they will prolong your life many years and bring you peace and prosperity. Let love and faithfulness never leave you; bind them around your neck, write them on the tablet of your heart.

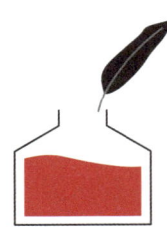

Day 08
愛不虛假 Love without Affectation

(Romans; Chapter 12: Verse 9-11)

⁹ Love must be sincere. Hate what is evil; cling to what is good. ¹⁰ Be devoted to one another in love. Honor one another above yourselves. ¹¹ Never be lacking in zeal, but keep your spiritual fervor, serving the Lord.

（羅馬書；12章，9-11節）

⁹ 愛人不可虛假；惡要厭惡，善要親近。¹⁰ 愛弟兄，要彼此親熱；恭敬人，要彼此推讓。¹¹ 殷勤不可懶惰。要心裡火熱，常常服事主。

Vocabulary

sincere [sɪnˈsɪr] adj. 真誠的	evil [ˈiːvəl] adj. 邪惡的
cling [klɪŋ] v. 緊抓	devoted [dɪˈvotɪd] adj. 摯愛的，忠誠的
honor [ˈɑːnɚ] v. 尊敬	above [əˈbʌv] prep. 在…之上
lacking [ˈlækɪŋ] adj. 缺乏	zeal [ziːl] n. 熱情
spiritual [ˈspɪrɪtʃuəl] adj. 精神上的	fervor [ˈfɜːvɚ] n. 熱忱

Love must be sincere. Hate what is evil; cling to what is good. Be devoted to one another in love. Honor one another above yourselves. Never be lacking in zeal, but keep your spiritual fervor, serving the Lord.

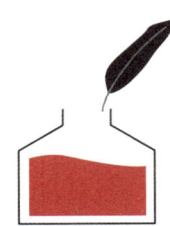

Day 09
愛無懼怕 Love without Fear

Day009.mp3

(1 John; Chapter 4: Verse 18-20)

¹⁸ There is no fear in love. But perfect love drives out fear, because fear has to do with punishment. The one who fears is not made perfect in love. ¹⁹ We love because he first loved us. ²⁰ Whoever claims to love God yet hates a brother or sister is a liar. For whoever does not love their brother and sister, whom they have seen, cannot love God, whom they have not seen.

（約翰一書；4章，18-20節）

¹⁸愛裡沒有懼怕；愛既完全，就把懼怕除去。因為懼怕裡含著刑罰，懼怕的人在愛裡未得完全。¹⁹我們愛，因為神先愛我們。²⁰人若說我愛神，卻恨他的弟兄，就是說謊話的；不愛他所看見的弟兄，就不能愛沒有看見的神（有古卷作：怎能愛沒有看見的神呢）。

Vocabulary

drives out 驅逐	have to do with 與⋯有關
whoever [huˈɛvɚ] pron. 無論誰	claim [klem] v. 聲稱
liar [ˈlaɪɚ] n. 撒謊者	yet [jɛt] adv. 然而

There is no fear in love. But perfect love drives out fear, because fear has to do with punishment. The one who fears is not made perfect in love. We love because he first loved us. Whoever claims to love God yet hates a brother or sister is a liar. For whoever does not love their brother and sister, whom they have seen, cannot love God, whom they have not seen.

Day 10
愛的全德 Love in Perfect Unity

(Colossians; Chapter 3: Verse 14-15)

¹⁴ And over all these virtues put on love, which binds them all together in perfect unity. ¹⁵ Let the peace of Christ rule in your hearts, since as members of one body you were called to peace. And be thankful.

（歌羅西書；3章，14-15節）

¹⁴ 在這一切之外，要存著愛心，愛心就是聯絡全德的。¹⁵ 又要叫基督的平安在你們心裡作主；你們也為此蒙召，歸為一體；且要存感謝的心。

Vocabulary

virtue [ˈvɝːtʃu] **n.** 美德	bind [baɪnd] **v.** 綁住，團結，聯合
perfect [ˈpɝːfɪkt] **adj.** 完美的	unity [ˈjuːnəti] **n.** 團結
rule [ruːl] **v.** 支配	body [ˈbɑːdi] **n.** 群體
call [kɔːl] **v.** 召喚	thankful [ˈθæŋkfəl] **adj.** 感激的

And over all these virtues put on love, which binds them all together in perfect unity. Let the peace of Christ rule in your hearts, since as members of one body you were called to peace. And be thankful.

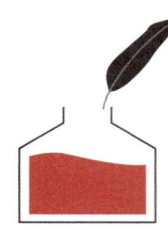

Day 11
愛的照顧 Care the Least Ones

Day011.mp3

(Matthew; Chapter 25: Verse 37-40)

³⁷ "Then the righteous will answer him, 'Lord, when did we see you hungry and feed you, or thirsty and give you something to drink? ³⁸ When did we see you a stranger and invite you in, or needing clothes and clothe you? ³⁹ When did we see you sick or in prison and go to visit you?' ⁴⁰ "The King will reply, 'Truly I tell you, whatever you did for one of the least of these brothers and sisters of mine, you did for me.'

（馬太福音；25 章，37-40 節）

³⁷ 義人就回答說：『主啊，我們什麼時候見祢餓了，給祢吃，渴了，給祢喝？ ³⁸ 什麼時候見祢作客旅，留祢住，或是赤身露體，給祢穿？ ³⁹ 又什麼時候見祢病了，或是在監裡，來看祢呢？』 ⁴⁰ 王要回答說：『我實在告訴你們，這些事你們既做在我這弟兄中一個最小的身上，就是做在我身上了。』

Vocabulary

righteous [ˈraɪtʃəs] **adj.** 正義的	hungry [ˈhʌngri] **adj.** 飢餓的
feed [fiːd] **v.** 餵養	thirsty [ˈθɝːsti] **adj.** 口渴的
stranger [ˈstreɪndʒɚ] **n.** 陌生人	invite [ɪnˈvaɪt] **v.** 邀請
clothes [kloʊðz] **n.** 衣服	clothe [kloʊð] **v.** 給…穿衣服
sick [sɪk] **adj.** 生病	prison [ˈprɪzn] **n.** 監獄

"Then the righteous will answer him, 'Lord, when did we see you hungry and feed you, or thirsty and give you something to drink? When did we see you a stranger and invite you in, or needing clothes and clothe you? When did we see you sick or in prison and go to visit you?' "The King will reply, 'Truly I tell you, whatever you did for one of the least of these brothers and sisters of mine, you did for me.'

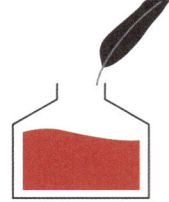

Day 12
愛的激勵 Love Compels Us

Day012.mp3

(2 Corinthians; Chapter 5: Verse 14-15)

14 For Christ's love compels us, because we are convinced that one died for all, and therefore all died. **15** And he died for all, that those who live should no longer live for themselves but for him who died for them and was raised again.

（哥林多後書；5章，14-15節）

14 原來基督的愛激勵我們；因我們想，一人既替眾人死，眾人就都死了；**15** 並且他替眾人死，是叫那些活著的人不再為自己活，乃為替他們死而復活的主活。

Vocabulary

compel [kəmˈpɛl] **v.** 強迫
therefore [ˈðɛrˌfɔːr] **adv.** 因此
raise [reɪz] **v.** 養育

convince [kənˈvɪns] **v.** 說服
no longer 不再

For Christ's love compels us, because we are convinced that one died for all, and therefore all died. And he died for all, that those who live should no longer live for themselves but for him who died for them and was raised again.

Day 13
愛的犧牲 Love's Sacrifice

(1 Thessalonians; Chapter 2: Verse 8-9)

⁸ so we cared for you. Because we loved you so much, we were delighted to share with you not only the gospel of God but our lives as well. ⁹ Surely you remember, brothers and sisters, our toil and hardship; we worked night and day in order not to be a burden to anyone while we preached the gospel of God to you.

（帖撒羅尼迦前書；2 章，8-9 節）

⁸ 我們既是這樣愛你們，不但願意將神的福音給你們，連自己的性命也願意給你們，因你們是我們所疼愛的。⁹ 弟兄們，你們記念我們的辛苦勞碌，晝夜做工，傳神的福音給你們，免得叫你們一人受累。

Vocabulary

care for v. 照顧，喜愛	delighted [dɪˈlaɪtɪd] adj. 愉快的
share [ʃɛr] v. 分享	gospel [ˈgɑːspəl] n. 福音
toil [tɔɪl] n. 辛勞	hardship [ˈhɑːrdʃɪp] n. 苦難
night and day 日以繼夜	in order not to 為了不
burden [ˈbɝːdn] n. 負擔	preach [priːtʃ] v. 傳講

so we cared for you. Because we loved you so much, we were delighted to share with you not only the gospel of God but our lives as well. Surely you remember, brothers and sisters, our toil and hardship; we worked night and day in order not to be a burden to anyone while we preached the gospel of God to you.

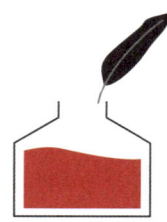

Day 14
愛你仇敵 Love Your Enemies

(Matthew; Chapter 5: Verse 43-45)

⁴³ "You have heard that it was said, 'Love your neighbor and hate your enemy.' ⁴⁴ But I tell you, love your enemies and pray for those who persecute you, ⁴⁵ that you may be children of your Father in heaven. He causes his sun to rise on the evil and the good, and sends rain on the righteous and the unrighteous.

（馬太福音；5章，43-45節）

⁴³ 你們聽見有話說：當愛你的鄰舍，恨你的仇敵。⁴⁴ 只是我告訴你們，要愛你們的仇敵，為那逼迫你們的禱告。⁴⁵ 這樣就可以作你們天父的兒子；因為祂叫日頭照好人，也照歹人；降雨給義人，也給不義的人。

Vocabulary

neighbor [ˈnebɚ] n. 鄰居
pray [pre] v. 祈禱
cause [ˈkɔːz] v. 造成
rise [raɪz] v. 上升
rain [ren] n. 雨
unrighteous [ˌʌnˈraɪtʃəs] adj. 不義的

enemy [ˈɛnəmi] n. 敵人
persecute [ˈpɝːsɪkjuːt] v. 迫害，逼迫，煩擾
sun [sʌn] n. 太陽
send [sɛnd] v. 傳送
righteous [ˈraɪtʃəs] adj. 正義的

36

"You have heard that it was said, 'Love your neighbor and hate your enemy.' But I tell you, love your enemies and pray for those who persecute you, that you may be children of your Father in heaven. He causes his sun to rise on the evil and the good, and sends rain on the righteous and the unrighteous.

Day 15
博愛大眾 Love Everyone

(Matthew; Chapter 5: Verse 46-48)

⁴⁶ If you love those who love you, what reward will you get? Are not even the tax collectors doing that? ⁴⁷ And if you greet only your own people, what are you doing more than others? Do not even pagans do that? ⁴⁸ Be perfect, therefore, as your heavenly Father is perfect.

（馬太福音；5 章，46-48 節）

⁴⁶ 你們若單愛那愛你們的人，有什麼賞賜呢？就是稅吏不也是這樣行嗎？⁴⁷ 你們若單請你弟兄的安，比人有什麼長處呢？就是外邦人不也是這樣行嗎？⁴⁸ 所以，你們要完全，像你們的天父完全一樣。

Vocabulary

reward [rɪˈwɔːrd] **n.** 獎勵
tax collector **n.** 稅吏
more than 多於
perfect [ˈpɝːfɪkt] **adj.** 完美的
heavenly [ˈhɛvənlɪ] **adj.** 天上的，天堂的

even [ˈiːvən] **adv.** 甚至
greet [griːt] **v.** 問候
pagan [ˈpeɡən] **n.** 異教徒
as [æz] **conj.** 如同

If you love those who love you, what reward will you get? Are not even the tax collectors doing that? And if you greet only your own people, what are you doing more than others? Do not even pagans do that? Be perfect, therefore, as your heavenly Father is perfect.

自我反思

我們一起完成了仁愛篇 15 天的閱讀與抄寫,現在就透過以下問題來看看各位所獲得的成果。

- 在仁愛篇中,最令您印象深刻的金句是哪一句?

  _____
  _____
  _____
  _____

- 這 15 天的單元中,您最喜歡哪一天的內容?為什麼?

  _____
  _____
  _____
  _____

Chapter 2
喜樂

(Proverbs; Chapter 15: Verse 13)

13 A happy heart makes the face cheerful, but heartache crushes the spirit.

（箴言；15章，13節）

13 心中喜樂，面帶笑容；心裡憂愁，靈被損傷。

Chapter2.mp3

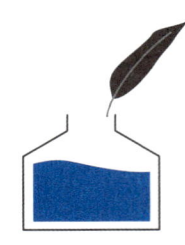

Day 16
靠主得喜樂 Rejoice in the LORD

(Philippians; Chapter 4: Verse 4-7)

4 Rejoice in the Lord always. I will say it again: Rejoice! **5** Let your gentleness be evident to all. The Lord is near. **6** Do not be anxious about anything, but in every situation, by prayer and petition, with thanksgiving, present your requests to God. **7** And the peace of God, which transcends all understanding, will guard your hearts and your minds in Christ Jesus.

（腓立比書；4章，4-7節）

4 你們要靠主常常喜樂。我再說，你們要喜樂。**5** 當叫眾人知道你們謙讓的心。主已經近了。**6** 應當一無掛慮，只要凡事藉著禱告、祈求，和感謝，將你們所要的告訴神。**7** 神所賜、出人意外的平安必在基督耶穌裡保守你們的心懷意念。

Vocabulary

rejoice [rɪˈdʒɔɪs] v. 歡欣	gentleness [ˈdʒɛntlnɪs] n. 溫柔
evident [ˈɛvɪdənt] adj. 明顯的	near [nɪr] adv. 接近
anxious [ˈæŋkʃəs] adj. 焦慮的	situation [ˌsɪtʃuˈeʃən] n. 情況
prayer [ˈprɛr] n. 禱告	petition [pəˈtɪʃən] n. 請願
present [ˈprɛzənt] v. 提出	request [rɪˈkwɛst] n. 請求
transcend [trænˈsɛnd] v. 超越	guard [gɑrd] v. 守護

Rejoice in the Lord always. I will say it again: Rejoice! Let your gentleness be evident to all. The Lord is near. Do not be anxious about anything, but in every situation, by prayer and petition, with thanksgiving, present your requests to God. And the peace of God, which transcends all understanding, will guard your hearts and your minds in Christ Jesus.

Day 17
喜樂的來源 The Source of Joy

(Psalm 42: Verse 5-6)

⁵ Why, my soul, are you downcast? Why so disturbed within me? Put your hope in God, for I will yet praise him, my Savior and my God. ⁶ My soul is downcast within me; therefore I will remember you from the land of the Jordan, the heights of Hermon—from Mount Mizar.

（詩篇；42 篇，5-6 節）

⁵ 我的心哪，你為何憂悶？為何在我裡面煩躁？應當仰望神，因祂笑臉幫助我；我還要稱讚祂。⁶ 我的神啊，我的心在我裡面憂悶，所以我從約但地，從黑門嶺，從米薩山記念祢。

Vocabulary

soul [sol] n. 心靈
disturbed [dɪˈstɝbd] adj. 不安的
praise [prez] v. 讚美
therefore [ˈðɛrˌfor] adv. 因此
land of the Jordan 約旦河地區
Mount Mizar 米薩山

downcast [ˈdaʊnkæst] adj. 沮喪的
hope [hop] n. 希望
within [wɪðˈɪn] prep. 在內部
remember [rɪˈmɛmbɚ] v. 記得
the heights of Hermon 黑門山高地

Why, my soul, are you downcast? Why so disturbed within me? Put your hope in God, for I will yet praise him, my Savior and my God. My soul is downcast within me; therefore I will remember you from the land of the Jordan, the heights of Hermon—from Mount Mizar.

Day 18

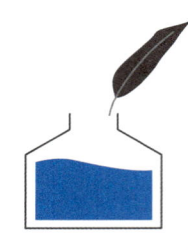

大大的喜樂
Rejoiced Greatly in the LORD

(Philippians; Chapter 4: Verse 10-11)

¹⁰ I rejoiced greatly in the Lord that at last you renewed your concern for me. Indeed, you were concerned, but you had no opportunity to show it. ¹¹ I am not saying this because I am in need, for I have learned to be content whatever the circumstances.

（腓立比書；4章，10-11節）

¹⁰ 我靠主大大的喜樂，因為你們思念我的心如今又發生；你們向來就思念我，只是沒得機會。¹¹ 我並不是因缺乏說這話；我無論在什麼景況都可以知足，這是我已經學會了。

Vocabulary

- **renew** [rɪˈnuː] **v.** 重新開始
- **indeed** [ɪnˈdiːd] **adv.** 確實
- **in need** 需要
- **content** [ˈkɑːntɛnt] **adj.** 滿足的
- **concern** [kənˈsɝːn] **n.** 掛念
- **opportunity** [ˌɑpɚˈtuːnɪti] **n.** 機會
- **learn** [ˈlɝːn] **v.** 學會
- **circumstance** [ˈsɝːkəmstæns] **n.** 情況

I rejoiced greatly in the Lord that at last you renewed your concern for me. Indeed, you were concerned, but you had no opportunity to show it. I am not saying this because I am in need, for I have learned to be content whatever the circumstances.

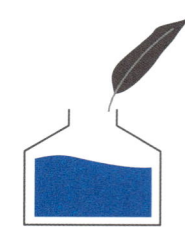

Day 19
不憂慮之樂 Do Not Worry

(Matthew; Chapter 6: Verse 31-32)

31 So do not worry, saying, 'What shall we eat?' or 'What shall we drink?' or 'What shall we wear?' **32** For the pagans run after all these things, and your heavenly Father knows that you need them.

（馬太福音；6 章，31-32 節）

31 所以，不要憂慮說：吃什麼？喝什麼？穿什麼？**32** 這都是外邦人所求的，你們需用的這一切東西，你們的天父是知道的。

Vocabulary

worry [ˈwɝːrɪ] **v.** 擔心
run after 追逐
need [niːd] **v.** 需要

pagan [ˈpegən] **n.** 異教徒
heavenly [ˈhɛvənlɪ] **adj.** 天上的

So do not worry, saying, 'What shall we eat?' or 'What shall we drink?' or 'What shall we wear?' For the pagans run after all these things, and your heavenly Father knows that you need them.

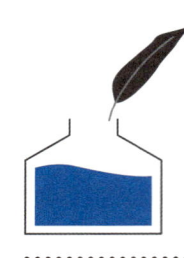

Day 20
滿足的喜樂 Fill with Joy

(Psalm 16: Verse 9-11)

⁹ Therefore my heart is glad and my tongue rejoices; my body also will rest secure, ¹⁰ because you will not abandon me to the realm of the dead, nor will you let your faithful one see decay. ¹¹ You make known to me the path of life; you will fill me with joy in your presence, with eternal pleasures at your right hand.

（詩篇；16 篇，9-11 節）

⁹ 因此，我的心歡喜，我的靈（原文是榮耀）快樂；我的肉身也要安然居住。¹⁰ 因為祢必不將我的靈魂撇在陰間，也不叫祢的聖者見朽壞。¹¹ 祢必將生命的道路指示我。在祢面前有滿足的喜樂；在祢右手中有永遠的福樂。

Vocabulary

fill [fɪl] v. 填滿
tongue [tʌŋ] n. 舌頭
secure [sɪˈkjʊr] adj. 安全的
realm [rɛlm] n. 領域，範圍
decay [dɪˈke] n. 腐壞
presence [ˈprɛzəns] n. 存在

glad [glæd] adj. 高興的
rest [rɛst] v. 休息
abandon [əˈbændən] v. 放棄
faithful [ˈfeθfəl] adj. 忠誠的
path [pæθ] n. 道路
eternal [ɪˈtɜːnl] adj. 永恆的

Therefore my heart is glad and my tongue rejoices; my body also will rest secure, because you will not abandon me to the realm of the dead, nor will you let your faithful one see decay. You make known to me the path of life; you will fill me with joy in your presence, with eternal pleasures at your right hand.

Day 21
患難中喜樂 Glory in Sufferings

(Romans; Chapter 5: Verse 3-5)

³ Not only so, but we also glory in our sufferings, because we know that suffering produces perseverance; ⁴ perseverance, character; and character, hope. ⁵ And hope does not put us to shame, because God's love has been poured out into our hearts through the Holy Spirit, who has been given to us.

（羅馬書；5章，3-5節）

³ 不但如此，就是在患難中也是歡歡喜喜的；因為知道患難生忍耐，⁴ 忍耐生老練，老練生盼望；⁵ 盼望不至於羞恥，因為所賜給我們的聖靈將神的愛澆灌在我們心裡。

Vocabulary

glory [ˈglɔri] n. 榮耀
produce [prəˈduːs] v. 產生
character [ˈkærɪktɚ] n. 性格
pour out 傾倒

suffering [ˈsʌfərɪŋ] n. 苦難
perseverance [ˌpɝːsəˈvɪrəns] n. 毅力
shame [ʃeɪm] n. 羞恥

Not only so, but we also glory in our sufferings, because we know that suffering produces perseverance; perseverance, character; and character, hope. And hope does not put us to shame, because God's love has been poured out into our hearts through the Holy Spirit, who has been given to us.

Day 22
試煉中喜樂 Face Trials with Joy

(James; Chapter 1: Verse 2-4)

² Consider it pure joy, my brothers and sisters, whenever you face trials of many kinds, ³ because you know that the testing of your faith produces perseverance. ⁴ Let perseverance finish its work so that you may be mature and complete, not lacking anything.

（雅各書；1章，2-4節）

² 我的弟兄們，你們落在百般試煉中，都要以為大喜樂；³ 因為知道你們的信心經過試驗，就生忍耐。⁴ 但忍耐也當成功，使你們成全、完備，毫無缺欠。

Vocabulary

consider [kənˈsɪdɚ] v. 考慮
joy [dʒɔɪ] n. 喜樂
trial [ˈtraɪəl] n. 試煉
mature [məˈtʃʊr] adj. 成熟的
lack [læk] v. 缺乏

pure [pjʊr] adj. 純淨的
face [fes] v. 面對
faith [feθ] n. 信心
complete [kəmˈpliːt] adj. 完全的

Consider it pure joy, my brothers and sisters, whenever you face trials of many kinds, because you know that the testing of your faith produces perseverance. Let perseverance finish its work so that you may be mature and complete, not lacking anything.

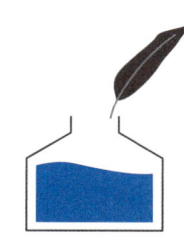

Day 23
喜樂的生活 Rejoice Always

(1 Thessalonians; Chapter 5: Verse 16-18)

16 Rejoice always, 17 pray continually, 18 give thanks in all circumstances; for this is God's will for you in Christ Jesus.

（帖撒羅尼迦前書；5章，16-18節）

16 要常常喜樂，17 不住的禱告，18 凡事謝恩；因為這是神在基督耶穌裡向你們所定的旨意。

Vocabulary

rejoice [rɪˈdʒɔɪs] v. 歡欣
continually [kənˈtɪnjuəli] adv. 不間斷地
for [fɔr] conj. 因為

pray [preɪ] v. 禱告
circumstance [ˈsɜːkəmstæns] n. 情況
will [wɪl] n. 意志

Rejoice always, pray continually, give thanks in all circumstances; for this is God's will for you in Christ Jesus.

Day 24
喜樂的同伴
Rejoice with Those Who Rejoice

(Romans; Chapter 12: Verse 15-17)

¹⁵ Rejoice with those who rejoice; mourn with those who mourn. ¹⁶ Live in harmony with one another. Do not be proud, but be willing to associate with people of low position. Do not be conceited. ¹⁷ Do not repay anyone evil for evil. Be careful to do what is right in the eyes of everyone.

（羅馬書；12章，15-17節）

¹⁵ 與喜樂的人要同樂；與哀哭的人要同哭。¹⁶ 要彼此同心；不要志氣高大，倒要俯就卑微的人（人：或作事）；不要自以為聰明。¹⁷ 不要以惡報惡；眾人以為美的事要留心去做。

Vocabulary

mourn [mɔrn] v. 哀悼	harmony [ˈhɑrmənɪ] n. 和諧
willing [ˈwɪlɪŋ] adj. 願意的	associate [əˈsoʃɪˌet] v. 與⋯交往
low position 卑微的地位	conceited [kənˈsiːtɪd] adj. 自負的
repay [rɪˈpeɪ] v. 償還	evil [ˈiːvəl] n./adj. 邪惡

Rejoice with those who rejoice; mourn with those who mourn. Live in harmony with one another. Do not be proud, but be willing to associate with people of low position. Do not be conceited. Do not repay anyone evil for evil. Be careful to do what is right in the eyes of everyone.

Day 25
喜樂的歡呼 Shouts of Joy

(Job; Chapter 8: Verse 20-22)

²⁰ "Surely God does not reject one who is blameless or strengthen the hands of evildoers. ²¹ He will yet fill your mouth with laughter and your lips with shouts of joy. ²² Your enemies will be clothed in shame, and the tents of the wicked will be no more."

（約伯記；8 章，20-22 節）

²⁰ 神必不丟棄完全人，也不扶助邪惡人。²¹ 他還要以喜笑充滿你的口，以歡呼充滿你的嘴。²² 恨惡你的要披戴慚愧；惡人的帳棚必歸於無有。

Vocabulary

shout [ʃaʊt] **n.** 呼喊	surely [ˈʃʊrli] **adv.** 必然
reject [rɪˈdʒɛkt] **v.** 拒絕	blameless [ˈbleɪmlɪs] **adj.** 無可指責的
strengthen [ˈstrɛŋθən] **v.** 加強	evildoer [ˈiːvəlˌduːɚ] **n.** 作惡者
laughter [ˈlæftɚ] **n.** 笑聲	lips [lɪps] **n.** 嘴唇
enemy [ˈɛnəmi] **n.** 敵人	clothe [kloʊð] **v.** 穿上
shame [ʃeɪm] **n.** 羞恥	tent [tɛnt] **n.** 帳篷
wicked [ˈwɪkɪd] **adj.** 邪惡的	

"Surely God does not reject one who is blameless or strengthen the hands of evildoers. He will yet fill your mouth with laughter and your lips with shouts of joy. Your enemies will be clothed in shame, and the tents of the wicked will be no more."

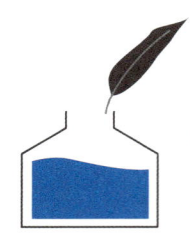

Day 26
喜樂與平安 Joy and Peace

(Romans; Chapter 15: Verse 13)

13 May the God of hope fill you with all joy and peace as you trust in him, so that you may overflow with hope by the power of the Holy Spirit.

（羅馬書；15章，13節）

13 但願使人有盼望的神，因信將諸般的喜樂、平安充滿你們的心，使你們藉著聖靈的能力大有盼望。

Vocabulary

may [me] 但願

joy [dʒɔɪ] n. 喜樂

trust [trʌst] v. 信任

power [ˈpaʊɚ] n. 能力

fill [fɪl] v. 填滿

peace [piːs] n. 平安

overflow [ˌovɚˈflo] v. 充滿

May the God of hope fill you with all joy and peace as you trust in him, so that you may overflow with hope by the power of the Holy Spirit.

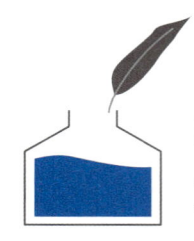

Day 27
喜樂與思想
Be Happy and Be Thoughtful

(Ecclesiastes; Chapter 7: Verse 13-14)

¹³ Consider what God has done: Who can straighten what he has made crooked? ¹⁴ When times are good, be happy; but when times are bad, consider this: God has made the one as well as the other. Therefore, no one can discover anything about their future.

（傳道書；7章，13-14節）

¹³ 你要察看神的作為；因神使為曲的，誰能變為直呢？¹⁴ 遇亨通的日子你當喜樂；遭患難的日子你當思想；因為神使這兩樣並列，為的是叫人查不出身後有什麼事。

Vocabulary

consider [kənˈsɪdɚ] v. 考慮
crooked [ˈkrʊkɪd] adj. 彎曲的
therefore [ˈðɛrfor] adv. 因此
discover [dɪsˈkʌvɚ] v. 發現

straighten [ˈstreɪtn] v. 使變直
as well as 以及
no one 沒有人
future [ˈfjuːtʃɚ] n. 未來

Consider what God has done: Who can straighten what he has made crooked? When times are good, be happy; but when times are bad, consider this: God has made the one as well as the other. Therefore, no one can discover anything about their future.

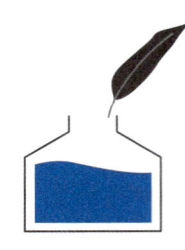

Day 28
喜樂與盼望 Joy and Hope

(1 Thessalonians; Chapter 2: Verse 19-20)

[19] For what is our hope, our joy, or the crown in which we will glory in the presence of our Lord Jesus when he comes? Is it not you? [20] Indeed, you are our glory and joy.

（帖撒羅尼迦前書；2 章，19-20 節）

[19] 我們的盼望和喜樂，並所誇的冠冕是什麼呢？豈不是我們主耶穌來的時候，你們在祂面前站立得住嗎？[20] 因為你們就是我們的榮耀，我們的喜樂。

Vocabulary

hope [hop] n. 盼望
crown [kraʊn] n. 冠冕
presence [ˈprɛzəns] n. 臨在

joy [dʒɔɪ] n. 喜樂
glory [ˈglɔrɪ] n. 榮耀
indeed [ɪnˈdiːd] adv. 的確

For what is our hope, our joy, or the crown in which we will glory in the presence of our Lord Jesus when he comes? Is it not you? Indeed, you are our glory and joy.

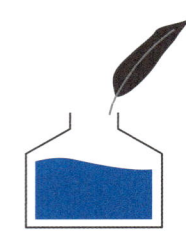

Day 29
喜樂為良藥
Cheerful Heart Is Good Medicine

(Proverbs; Chapter 17: Verse 22-24)

²² A cheerful heart is good medicine, but a crushed spirit dries up the bones. ²³ The wicked accept bribes in secret to pervert the course of justice. ²⁴ A discerning person keeps wisdom in view, but a fool's eyes wander to the ends of the earth.

（箴言；17 章，22-24 節）

²² 喜樂的心乃是良藥；憂傷的靈使骨枯乾。²³ 惡人暗中受賄賂，為要顛倒判斷。²⁴ 明哲人眼前有智慧；愚昧人眼望地極。

Vocabulary

cheerful [ˈtʃɪrfəl] adj. 開心的	medicine [ˈmɛdəsən] n. 藥
crushed [krʌʃt] adj. 極度傷心的	spirit [ˈspɪrɪt] n. 心靈
dry up 使乾枯	bone [boʊn] n. 骨頭
the wicked 惡人	accept [ækˈsɛpt] v. 接受
bribe [braɪb] n. 賄賂	pervert [pɚˈvɝt] v. 扭曲
justice [ˈdʒʌstɪs] n. 公義	discerning [dɪˈsɝnɪŋ] adj. 有洞察力的
wisdom [ˈwɪzdəm] n. 智慧	fool [fuːl] n. 愚人
wander [ˈwɑːndɚ] v. 遊蕩	

A cheerful heart is good medicine, but a crushed spirit dries up the bones. The wicked accept bribes in secret to pervert the course of justice. A discerning person keeps wisdom in view, but a fool's eyes wander to the ends of the earth.

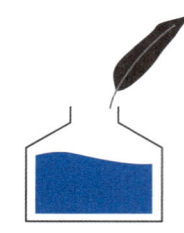

Day 30
喜樂過生活 Live in Joy

(Philippians; Chapter 4: Verse 12-13)

¹² I know what it is to be in need, and I know what it is to have plenty. I have learned the secret of being content in any and every situation, whether well fed or hungry, whether living in plenty or in want. ¹³ I can do all this through him who gives me strength.

（腓立比書；4章，12-13節）

¹² 我知道怎樣處卑賤，也知道怎樣處豐富；或飽足，或飢餓；或有餘，或缺乏，隨事隨在，我都得了祕訣。¹³ 我靠著那加給我力量的，凡事都能做。

Vocabulary

content [kənˈtɛnt] **adj.** 滿足的
in plenty 充足
strength [strɛŋθ] **n.** 力量
well fed 飽足
in want 貧乏

I know what it is to be in need, and I know what it is to have plenty. I have learned the secret of being content in any and every situation, whether well fed or hungry, whether living in plenty or in want. I can do all this through him who gives me strength.

自我反思

我們一起完成了喜樂篇 15 天的閱讀與抄寫,現在就透過以下問題來看看各位所獲得的成果。

- 在喜樂篇中,最令您印象深刻的金句是哪一句?

- 這 15 天的單元中,您最喜歡哪一天的內容?為什麼?

Chapter 3
和平

(Matthew; Chapter 5: Verse 9)

**9 Blessed are the peacemakers,
for they will be called children of God.**

（馬太福音；5章，9節）

9 使人和睦的人有福了！因為他們必稱為神的兒子。

Chapter3.mp3

Day 31
神國在乎和平
God's Kingdom Is a Matter of Peace

(Romans; Chapter 14: Verse 17-19)

¹⁷ For the kingdom of God is not a matter of eating and drinking, but of righteousness, peace and joy in the Holy Spirit, ¹⁸ because anyone who serves Christ in this way is pleasing to God and receives human approval. ¹⁹ Let us therefore make every effort to do what leads to peace and to mutual edification.

（羅馬書；14 章，17-19 節）

¹⁷ 因為神的國不在乎吃喝，只在乎公義、和平，並聖靈中的喜樂。¹⁸ 在這幾樣上服事基督的，就為神所喜悅，又為人所稱許。¹⁹ 所以，我們務要追求和睦的事與彼此建立德行的事。

Vocabulary

kingdom [ˈkɪŋdəm] n. 國度	righteousness [ˈraɪtʃəsnɪs] n. 公義
peace [piːs] n. 和平	joy [dʒɔɪ] n. 喜樂
spirit [ˈspɪrɪt] n. 靈	approval [əˈpruːvəl] n. 認可
effort [ˈɛfɚt] n. 努力	edification [ˌɛdəfəˈkeʃən] n. 建立
Christ [kraɪst] n. 基督	mutual [ˈmjuːtʃuəl] adj. 互相的

For the kingdom of God is not a matter of eating and drinking, but of righteousness, peace and joy in the Holy Spirit, because anyone who serves Christ in this way is pleasing to God and receives human approval. Let us therefore make every effort to do what leads to peace and to mutual edification.

Day 32
和平從上頭來 Peace from Heaven

(James; Chapter 3: Verse 16-18)

¹⁶ For where you have envy and selfish ambition, there you find disorder and every evil practice. ¹⁷ But the wisdom that comes from heaven is first of all pure; then peace-loving, considerate, submissive, full of mercy and good fruit, impartial and sincere. ¹⁸ Peacemakers who sow in peace reap a harvest of righteousness.

（雅各書；3章，16-18節）

¹⁶ 在何處有嫉妒、紛爭，就在何處有擾亂和各樣的壞事。¹⁷ 惟獨從上頭來的智慧，先是清潔，後是和平，溫良柔順，滿有憐憫，多結善果，沒有偏見，沒有假冒。¹⁸ 並且使人和平的，是用和平所栽種的義果。

Vocabulary

envy [ˈɛnvi] n. 嫉妒	ambition [æmˈbɪʃən] n. 野心
disorder [dɪsˈɔrdɚ] n. 混亂	evil [ˈivəl] adj. 邪惡的
wisdom [ˈwɪzdəm] n. 智慧	pure [pjʊr] adj. 純潔的
mercy [ˈmɝsi] n. 憐憫	impartial [ɪmˈparʃəl] adj. 公正的
sincere [sɪnˈsɪr] adj. 真誠的	harvest [ˈharvɪst] n. 收穫

For where you have envy and selfish ambition, there you find disorder and every evil practice. But the wisdom that comes from heaven is first of all pure; then peace-loving, considerate, submissive, full of mercy and good fruit, impartial and sincere. Peacemakers who sow in peace reap a harvest of righteousness.

Day 33
和平的君降生
Prince of Peace Is Given

(Isaiah; Chapter 9: Verse 6)

⁶ For to us a child is born, to us a son is given, and the government will be on his shoulders. And he will be called Wonderful Counselor, Mighty God, Everlasting Father, Prince of Peace.

（以賽亞書；9章，6節）

⁶ 因有一嬰孩為我們而生；有一子賜給我們。政權必擔在祂的肩頭上；祂名稱為奇妙策士、全能的神、永在的父、和平的君。

Vocabulary

- child [tʃaɪld] **n.** 孩子
- government [ˈgʌvənmənt] **n.** 政權
- wonderful [ˈwʌndəfəl] **adj.** 奇妙的
- mighty [ˈmaɪtɪ] **adj.** 強大的
- father [ˈfɑðə] **n.** 父親
- son [sʌn] **n.** 兒子
- shoulder [ˈʃoʊldə] **n.** 肩膀
- counselor [ˈkaʊnslə] **n.** 諮詢者
- everlasting [ˌɛvəˈlæstɪŋ] **adj.** 永恆的
- prince [prɪns] **n.** 王子

For to us a child is born, to us a son is given, and the government will be on his shoulders. And he will be called Wonderful Counselor, Mighty God, Everlasting Father, Prince of Peace.

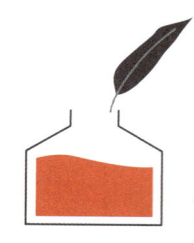

Day 34
傳揚和平福音
Come and Preach Peace

(Ephesians; Chapter 2: Verse 17-19)

¹⁷ He came and preached peace to you who were far away and peace to those who were near. ¹⁸ For through him we both have access to the Father by one Spirit. ¹⁹ Consequently, you are no longer foreigners and strangers, but fellow citizens with God's people and also members of his household,

（以弗所書；2章，17-19節）

¹⁷ 並且來傳和平的福音給你們遠處的人，也給那近處的人。¹⁸ 因為我們兩下藉著他被一個聖靈所感，得以進到父面前。¹⁹ 這樣，你們不再作外人和客旅，是與聖徒同國，是神家裡的人了

Vocabulary

preach [pritʃ] v. 傳講	peace [pis] n. 和平
far [far] adv. 遠	near [nɪr] adj. 近處
access [ˈæksɛs] n. 進入	stranger [ˈstrendʒɚ] n. 陌生人
citizen [ˈsɪtɪzən] n. 公民	household [ˈhaʊsˌhoʊld] n. 家庭

He came and preached peace to you who were far away and peace to those who were near. For through him we both have access to the Father by one Spirit. Consequently, you are no longer foreigners and strangers, but fellow citizens with God's people and also members of his household,

Day 35
同心追求和平 Pursue Peace

(2 Timothy; Chapter 2: Verse 22-23)

²² Flee the evil desires of youth and pursue righteousness, faith, love and peace, along with those who call on the Lord out of a pure heart. ²³ Don't have anything to do with foolish and stupid arguments, because you know they produce quarrels.

（提摩太後書；2章，22-23節）

²² 你要逃避少年的私慾，同那清心禱告主的人追求公義、信德、仁愛、和平。
²³ 惟有那愚拙無學問的辯論，總要棄絕，因為知道這等事是起爭競的。

Vocabulary

flee [fli] v. 逃避	desire [dɪˈzaɪɚ] n. 慾望
youth [juθ] n. 青春	pursue [pɚˈsu] v. 追求
righteousness [ˈraɪtʃəsnɪs] n. 公義	foolish [ˈfulɪʃ] adj. 愚蠢的
stupid [ˈstupɪd] adj. 愚笨的	argument [ˈɑrgjəmənt] n. 爭論
produce [prəˈdus] v. 產生	quarrel [ˈkwɔrəl] n. 爭吵

Flee the evil desires of youth and pursue righteousness, faith, love and peace, along with those who call on the Lord out of a pure heart. Don't have anything to do with foolish and stupid arguments, because you know they produce quarrels.

Day 36
不與他人相爭 Don't Accuse Others

(Proverbs; Chapter 3: Verse 30-32)

³⁰ Do not accuse anyone for no reason— when they have done you no harm. ³¹ Do not envy the violent or choose any of their ways. ³² For the Lord detests the perverse but takes the upright into his confidence.

（箴言；3章，30-32節）

³⁰ 人未曾加害與你、不可無故與他相爭。³¹ 不可嫉妒強暴的人、也不可選擇他所行的路。³² 因為乖僻人為耶和華所憎惡，正直人為祂所親密。

Vocabulary

accuse [əˈkjuz] v. 指控	anyone [ˈɛnɪˌwʌn] pron. 任何人
reason [ˈrizən] n. 理由	harm [harm] n. 傷害
envy [ˈɛnvi] v. 嫉妒	violent [ˈvaɪələnt] adj. 暴力的
choose [tʃuz] v. 選擇	perverse [pɚˈvɝs] adj. 倔強的
upright [ˈʌpˌraɪt] adj. 正直的	confidence [ˈkɑnfədəns] n. 信心

Do not accuse anyone for no reason— when they have done you no harm. Do not envy the violent or choose any of their ways. For the Lord detests the perverse but takes the upright into his confidence.

Day 37
追求與人和睦
Live in Peace with Everyone

(Hebrews; Chapter 12: Verse 14-16)

¹⁴ Make every effort to live in peace with everyone and to be holy; without holiness no one will see the Lord. ¹⁵ See to it that no one falls short of the grace of God and that no bitter root grows up to cause trouble and defile many. ¹⁶ See that no one is sexually immoral, or is Godless like Esau, who for a single meal sold his inheritance rights as the oldest son.

（希伯來書；12章，14-16節）

¹⁴ 你們要追求與眾人和睦，並要追求聖潔；非聖潔沒有人能見主。¹⁵ 又要謹慎，恐怕有人失了神的恩；恐怕有毒根生出來擾亂你們，因此叫眾人沾染污穢；¹⁶ 恐怕有淫亂的，有貪戀世俗如以掃的，他因一點食物把自己長子的名分賣了。

Vocabulary

effort [ˈɛfɚt] n. 努力	live [lɪv] v. 生活，過活
peace [pis] n. 和平	everyone [ˈɛvrɪˌwʌn] pron. 每個人
holy [ˈholi] adj. 神聖的	holiness [ˈholɪnɪs] n. 聖潔
grace [gres] n. 恩典	bitter [ˈbɪtɚ] adj. 苦澀的
trouble [ˈtrʌbəl] n. 麻煩	defile [dɪˈfaɪl] v. 汙染

Make every effort to live in peace with everyone and to be holy; without holiness no one will see the Lord. See to it that no one falls short of the grace of God and that no bitter root grows up to cause trouble and defile many. See that no one is sexually immoral, or is Godless like Esau, who for a single meal sold his inheritance rights as the oldest son.

Day 38
彼此不發怨言
Without Grumbling or Arguing

(1 Peter; Chapter 4: Verse 8-10)

⁸ Above all, love each other deeply, because love covers over a multitude of sins. ⁹ Offer hospitality to one another without grumbling. ¹⁰ Each of you should use whatever gift you have received to serve others, as faithful stewards of God's grace in its various forms.

（彼得前書；4章，8-10節）

⁸最要緊的是彼此切實相愛，因為愛能遮掩許多的罪。⁹你們要互相款待，不發怨言。¹⁰各人要照所得的恩賜彼此服事，作神百般恩賜的好管家。

Vocabulary

deeply [ˈdiplɪ] adv. 深刻地
multitude [ˈmʌltəˌtjud] n. 許多
grumble [ˈgrʌmbl] v. 抱怨
serve [sɝv] v. 服務
various [ˈvɛrɪəs] adj. 各樣的

cover [ˈkʌvɚ] v. 遮蓋
hospitality [ˌhɑspɪˈtælətɪ] n. 殷勤招待
gift [gɪft] v. 賜與，贈與
steward [ˈstjuwɚd] n. 管家
form [fɔrm] n. 形式

Above all, love each other deeply, because love covers over a multitude of sins. Offer hospitality to one another without grumbling. Each of you should use whatever gift you have received to serve others, as faithful stewards of God's grace in its various forms.

Day 39
務要彼此和睦
Live in Peace with Each Other

(2 Corinthians; Chapter 13: Verse 11-12)

¹¹ Finally, brothers and sisters, rejoice! Strive for full restoration, encourage one another, be of one mind, live in peace. And the God of love and peace will be with you. ¹² Greet one another with a holy kiss.

（哥林多後書；13 章，11-12 節）

¹¹ 還有末了的話：願弟兄們都喜樂。要作完全人；要受安慰；要同心合意；要彼此和睦。如此，仁愛和平的神必常與你們同在。¹² 你們親嘴問安，彼此務要聖潔。

Vocabulary

finally [ˈfaɪnəlɪ] adv. 最後	rejoice [rɪˈdʒɔɪs] v. 歡欣
strive [straɪv] v. 努力	restoration [ˌrɛstəˈreʃən] n. 恢復
encourage [ɪnˈkɝɪdʒ] v. 鼓勵	peace [pis] n. 和平
love [lʌv] n. 愛	greet [grit] v. 問候
kiss [kɪs] n. 親吻	

Finally, brothers and sisters, rejoice! Strive for full restoration, encourage one another, be of one mind, live in peace. And the God of love and peace will be with you. Greet one another with a holy kiss.

Day 40
不與弟兄動怒
Don't Be Angry with Others

(Matthew; Chapter 5: Verse 21-22)

21 "You have heard that it was said to the people long ago, 'You shall not murder, and anyone who murders will be subject to judgment.' 22 But I tell you that anyone who is angry with a brother or sister will be subject to judgment. Again, anyone who says to a brother or sister, 'Raca,' is answerable to the court. And anyone who says, 'You fool!' will be in danger of the fire of hell.

（馬太福音；5 章，21-22 節）

21 你們聽見有吩咐古人的話，說：不可殺人；又說：凡殺人的難免受審判。22 只是我告訴你們：凡（有古卷在凡字下加：無緣無故地）向弟兄動怒的，難免受審斷；凡罵弟兄是拉加的，難免公會的審斷；凡罵弟兄是魔利的，難免地獄的火。

Vocabulary

heard [hɝd] v.（hear 的過去式）聽見	murder [ˈmɝdɚ] v., n. 謀殺
subject [ˈsʌbˌdʒɛkt] adj., n. 服從	judgment [ˈdʒʌdʒmənt] n. 判決
angry [ˈæŋgrɪ] adj. 生氣的	brother [ˈbrʌðɚ] n. 兄弟
sister [ˈsɪstɚ] n. 姊妹	court [kɔrt] n. 法庭
fool [ful] n. 愚人	danger [ˈdendʒɚ] n. 危險

"You have heard that it was said to the people long ago, 'You shall not murder, and anyone who murders will be subject to judgment.' But I tell you that anyone who is angry with a brother or sister will be subject to judgment. Again, anyone who says to a brother or sister, 'Raca,' is answerable to the court. And anyone who says, 'You fool!' will be in danger of the fire of hell.

Day 41
無限饒恕弟兄
Forgive Seventy-seven Times

(Matthew; Chapter 18: Verse 21-22)

²¹ Then Peter came to Jesus and asked, "Lord, how many times shall I forgive my brother or sister who sins against me? Up to seven times?" ²² Jesus answered, "I tell you, not seven times, but seventy-seven times.

（馬太福音；18 章，21-22 節）

²¹ 那時，彼得進前來，對耶穌說：主啊，我弟兄得罪我，我當饒恕他幾次呢？到七次可以嗎？ ²² 耶穌說：我對你說，不是到七次，乃是到七十個七次。

Vocabulary

ask [æsk] v. 問

sin [sɪn] n. 罪

seven [ˈsɛvən] n. 七

seventy-seven [ˈsɛvənˌti sɛvən] 七十七

forgive [fəˈgɪv] v. 原諒

against [əˈgɛnst] prep. 反對

answer [ˈænsə] v. 回答

Then Peter came to Jesus and asked, "Lord, how many times shall I forgive my brother or sister who sins against me? Up to seven times?" Jesus answered, "I tell you, not seven times, but seventy-seven times.

Day 42
弟兄和睦同居
Live Together in Unity

(Psalm 133: Verse 1-3)

¹ How good and pleasant it is when God's people live together in unity! ² It is like precious oil poured on the head, running down on the beard, running down on Aaron's beard, down on the collar of his robe. ³ It is as if the dew of Hermon were falling on Mount Zion. For there the Lord bestows his blessing, even life forevermore.

（詩篇 133 篇，1-3 節）

¹ 看哪，弟兄和睦同居是何等地善，何等地美！² 這好比那貴重的油澆在亞倫的頭上，流到鬍鬚，又流到他的衣襟；³ 又好比黑門的甘露降在錫安山；因為在那裡有耶和華所命定的福，就是永遠的生命。

Vocabulary

- good [gʊd] **adj.** 好的
- unity [ˈjuːnəti] **n.** 團結
- oil [ɔɪl] **n.** 油
- collar [ˈkɑːlə] **n.** 衣領
- blessing [ˈblɛsɪŋ] **n.** 祝福
- pleasant [ˈplɛzənt] **adj.** 愉快的
- precious [ˈprɛʃəs] **adj.** 珍貴的
- beard [bɪrd] **n.** 鬍鬚
- robe [rob] **n.** 長袍
- forevermore [fəˈɛvəmor] **adv.** 永遠

How good and pleasant it is when God's people live together in unity! It is like precious oil poured on the head, running down on the beard, running down on Aaron's beard, down on the collar of his robe. It is as if the dew of Hermon were falling on Mount Zion. For there the Lord bestows his blessing, even life forevermore.

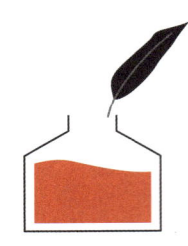

Day 43
不要以惡報惡
Don't Repay Evil with Evil

(1 Peter; Chapter 3: Verse 9-11)

⁹ Do not repay evil with evil or insult with insult. On the contrary, repay evil with blessing, because to this you were called so that you may inherit a blessing. ¹⁰ For, "Whoever would love life and see good days must keep their tongue from evil and their lips from deceitful speech. ¹¹ They must turn from evil and do good; they must seek peace and pursue it.

（彼得前書；3章，9-11節）

⁹ 不以惡報惡，以辱罵還辱罵，倒要祝福；因你們是為此蒙召，好叫你們承受福氣。¹⁰ 因為經上說：人若愛生命，願享美福，須要禁止舌頭不出惡言，嘴唇不說詭詐的話；¹¹ 也要離惡行善；尋求和睦，一心追趕。

Vocabulary

repay [rɪˈpe] v. 償還
insult [ˈɪnsʌlt] n. 侮辱
inherit [ɪnˈhɛrɪt] v. 繼承
deceitful [dɪˈsiːtfəl] adj. 欺騙的
pursue [pɚˈsuː] v. 追求

evil [ˈiːvəl] n. 邪惡
blessing [ˈblɛsɪŋ] n. 祝福
tongue [tʌŋ] n. 舌頭
seek [siːk] v. 尋求

Do not repay evil with evil or insult with insult. On the contrary, repay evil with blessing, because to this you were called so that you may inherit a blessing. For, "Whoever would love life and see good days must keep their tongue from evil and their lips from deceitful speech. They must turn from evil and do good; they must seek peace and pursue it.

Day 44
善待你的仇敵
Be Kind to Your Enemy

(Romans; Chapter 12: Verse 20-21)

[20] On the contrary: "If your enemy is hungry, feed him; if he is thirsty, give him something to drink. In doing this, you will heap burning coals on his head." [21] Do not be overcome by evil, but overcome evil with good.

（羅馬書；12章，20-21節）

[20] 所以，你的仇敵若餓了，就給他吃，若渴了，就給他喝；因為你這樣行就是把炭火堆在他的頭上。[21] 你不可為惡所勝，反要以善勝惡。

Vocabulary

enemy [ˈɛnəmɪ] n. 敵人	hungry [ˈhʌŋgrɪ] adj. 飢餓的
feed [fiːd] v. 餵食	thirsty [ˈθɝstɪ] adj. 口渴的
drink [drɪŋk] v. 喝	overcome [ˌovɚˈkʌm] v. 克服
good [gʊd] adj. 好的	burning [ˈbɝnɪŋ] adj. 燃燒的
coal [kol] n. 煤炭	

On the contrary: "If your enemy is hungry, feed him; if he is thirsty, give him something to drink. In doing this, you will heap burning coals on his head." Do not be overcome by evil, but overcome evil with good.

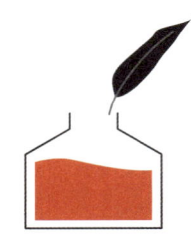

Day 45
與仇敵和好
Make Peace with Enemies

(Proverbs; Chapter 16: Verse 5-7)

⁵ The Lord detests all the proud of heart. Be sure of this: They will not go unpunished. ⁶ Through love and faithfulness sin is atoned for; through the fear of the Lord evil is avoided. ⁷ When the Lord takes pleasure in anyone's way, he causes their enemies to make peace with them.

（箴言；16章，5-7節）

⁵ 凡心裡驕傲的，為耶和華所憎惡；雖然連手，他必不免受罰。⁶ 因憐憫誠實、罪孽得贖；敬畏耶和華的、遠離惡事。⁷ 人所行的若蒙耶和華喜悅、耶和華也使他的仇敵與他和好。

Vocabulary

detest [dɪˈtɛst] v. 厭惡
heart [hɑrt] n. 心
faithfulness [ˈfeɪθfəlnəs] n. 忠誠
avoide [əˈvɔɪd] v. 避免
make [mek] v. 使

proud [praʊd] adj. 驕傲的
punish [ˈpʌnɪʃ] v. 懲罰
atone [əˈtoʊn] v. 贖罪
pleasure [ˈplɛʒɚ] n. 喜悅

The Lord detests all the proud of heart. Be sure of this: They will not go unpunished. Through love and faithfulness sin is atoned for; through the fear of the Lord evil is avoided. When the Lord takes pleasure in anyone's way, he causes their enemies to make peace with them.

自我反思

我們一起完成了和平篇 15 天的閱讀與抄寫,現在就透過以下問題來看看各位所獲得的成果。

- 在和平篇中,最令您印象深刻的金句是哪一句?

- 這 15 天的單元中,您最喜歡哪一天的內容?為什麼?

Chapter 4
忍耐

(2 Thessalonians; Chapter 3: Verse 5)

⁵ May the Lord direct your hearts into God's love and Christ's perseverance.

（帖撒羅尼迦後書；3章，5節）

⁵ 願主引導你們的心，叫你們愛神，並學基督的忍耐。

Chapter4.mp3

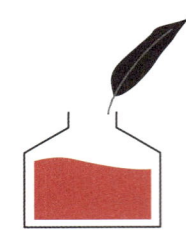

Day 46
效法耶穌忍耐
Learn from Jesus's Endurance

(Romans; Chapter 15: Verse 4-5)

⁴ For everything that was written in the past was written to teach us, so that through the endurance taught in the Scriptures and the encouragement they provide we might have hope. ⁵ May the God who gives endurance and encouragement give you the same attitude of mind toward each other that Christ Jesus had,

（羅馬書；15章，4-5節）

⁴ 從前所寫的聖經都是為教訓我們寫的，叫我們因聖經所生的忍耐和安慰可以得著盼望。⁵ 但願賜忍耐安慰的神叫你們彼此同心，效法基督耶穌，

Vocabulary

everything [ˈɛvrɪˌθɪŋ] pron. 一切
teach [titʃ] v. 教導
Scriptures [ˈskrɪptʃɚz] n. 聖經
provide [prəˈvaɪd] v. 提供
attitude [ˈætətjud] n. 態度

written [ˈrɪtn] v.（write 的過去分詞）（被）書寫
endurance [ɪnˈdʊrəns] n. 忍耐
encouragement [ɪnˈkɝɪdʒmənt] n. 鼓勵
hope [hoʊp] n. 希望

For everything that was written in the past was written to teach us, so that through the endurance taught in the Scriptures and the encouragement they provide we might have hope. May the God who gives endurance and encouragement give you the same attitude of mind toward each other that Christ Jesus had,

Day 47

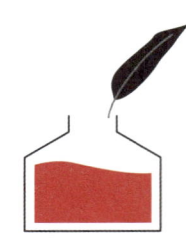

忍耐行神旨意
Persevere till God's Will Is Done

(Hebrews; Chapter 10: Verse 36-37)

36 You need to persevere so that when you have done the will of God, you will receive what he has promised. **37** For, "In just a little while, he who is coming will come and will not delay."

（希伯來書；10 章，36-37 節）

36 你們必須忍耐，使你們行完了神的旨意，就可以得著所應許的。**37** 因為還有一點點時候，那要來的就來，並不遲延；

Vocabulary

- **need** [nid] **v.** 需要
- **receive** [rɪˈsiv] **v.** 接受
- **delay** [dɪˈle] **v.** 延遲
- **persevere** [ˌpɝ-səˈvɪr] **v.** 堅持
- **promise** [ˈprɑmɪs] **v.** 承諾

You need to persevere so that when you have done the will of God, you will receive what he has promised. For, "In just a little while, he who is coming will come and will not delay."

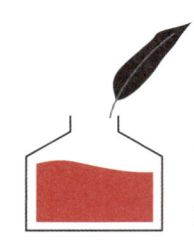

Day 48
忍耐不覺受苦
Glory Overcomes Present Sufferings

(Romans; Chapter 8: Verse 16-18)

¹⁶ The Spirit himself testifies with our spirit that we are God's children. ¹⁷ Now if we are children, then we are heirs—heirs of God and co-heirs with Christ, if indeed we share in his sufferings in order that we may also share in his glory. ¹⁸ I consider that our present sufferings are not worth comparing with the glory that will be revealed in us.

（羅馬書；8 章，16-18 節）

¹⁶ 聖靈與我們的心同證我們是神的兒女；¹⁷ 既是兒女，便是後嗣，就是神的後嗣，和基督同作後嗣。如果我們和他一同受苦，也必和他一同得榮耀。¹⁸ 我想，現在的苦楚若比起將來要顯於我們的榮耀就不足介意了。

Vocabulary

spirit [ˈspɪrɪt] n. 靈	testify [ˈtɛstəˌfaɪ] v. 證明
children [ˈtʃɪldrən] n. 兒女	heir [ɛr] n. 繼承人
suffering [ˈsʌfə-ɪŋ] n. 苦難	glory [ˈglɔri] n. 榮耀
present [ˈprɛzənt] adj. 當下的	reveal [rɪˈvil] v. 顯露

The Spirit himself testifies with our spirit that we are God's children. Now if we are children, then we are heirs—heirs of God and co-heirs with Christ, if indeed we share in his sufferings in order that we may also share in his glory. I consider that our present sufferings are not worth comparing with the glory that will be revealed in us.

Day 49
忍耐受苦榜樣 Example of Patience

(James; Chapter 5: Verse 10-11)

10 Brothers and sisters, as an example of patience in the face of suffering, take the prophets who spoke in the name of the Lord. **11** As you know, we count as blessed those who have persevered. You have heard of Job's perseverance and have seen what the Lord finally brought about. The Lord is full of compassion and mercy.

（雅各書；5章，10-11節）

10 弟兄們，你們要把那先前奉主名說話的眾先知當作能受苦能忍耐的榜樣。**11** 那先前忍耐的人，我們稱他們是有福的。你們聽見過約伯的忍耐，也知道主給他的結局，明顯主是滿心憐憫，大有慈悲。

Vocabulary

example [ɪɡˈzæmpəl] n. 例子
patience [ˈpeʃəns] n. 忍耐
suffering [ˈsʌfəɪŋ] n. 苦難
prophet [ˈprɑfɪt] n. 先知
compassion [kəmˈpæʃən] n. 憐憫
mercy [ˈmɝsɪ] n. 慈悲
blessed [ˈblɛst] adj. 有福的

Brothers and sisters, as an example of patience in the face of suffering, take the prophets who spoke in the name of the Lord. As you know, we count as blessed those who have persevered. You have heard of Job's perseverance and have seen what the Lord finally brought about. The Lord is full of compassion and mercy.

Day 50
忍耐以致結實
By Persevering Produce a Crop

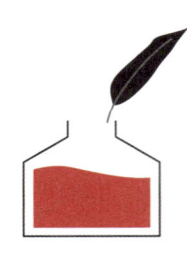

(Luke; Chapter 8: Verse 14-15)

¹⁴ The seed that fell among thorns stands for those who hear, but as they go on their way they are choked by life's worries, riches and pleasures, and they do not mature. ¹⁵ But the seed on good soil stands for those with a noble and good heart, who hear the word, retain it, and by persevering produce a crop.

（路加福音；8章，14-15節）

¹⁴ 那落在荊棘裡的，就是人聽了道，走開以後，被今生的思慮、錢財、宴樂擠住了，便結不出成熟的子粒來。¹⁵ 那落在好土裡的，就是人聽了道，持守在誠實善良的心裡，並且忍耐著結實。

Vocabulary

seed [sid] n. 種子
thorn [θɔrn] n. 荊棘
choke [tʃok] v. 窒息
riches [ˈrɪtʃɪz] n. 財富
mature [məˈtjʊr] v. 成熟

fell [fɛl] v.（fall 的過去式）落下
hear [hɪr] v. 聽見
worry [ˈwɝi] n. 憂慮
pleasure [ˈplɛʒɚ] n. 快樂

The seed that fell among thorns stands for those who hear, but as they go on their way they are choked by life's worries, riches and pleasures, and they do not mature. But the seed on good soil stands for those with a noble and good heart, who hear the word, retain it, and by persevering produce a crop.

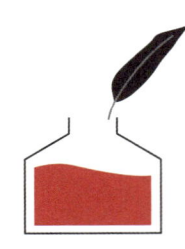

Day 51
忍耐必得開路
The Way to Endurance

(1 Corinthians; Chapter 10: Verse 13)

13 No temptation has overtaken you except what is common to mankind. And God is faithful; he will not let you be tempted beyond what you can bear. But when you are tempted, he will also provide a way out so that you can endure it.

（哥林多前書；10章，13節）

13 你們所遇見的試探，無非是人所能受的。神是信實的，必不叫你們受試探過於所能受的；在受試探的時候，總要給你們開一條出路，叫你們能忍受得住。

Vocabulary

temptation [tɛmpˈteʃən] **n.** 誘惑
common [ˈkɑmən] **adj.** 普通的
tempt [ˈtɛmpt] **v.** 誘惑
bear [bɛr] **v.** 忍受

overtake [ˌovɚˈtek] **v.** 超越
faithful [ˈfeθfəl] **adj.** 忠誠的
beyond [bɪˈjɑnd] **prep.** 超過

No temptation has overtaken you except what is common to mankind. And God is faithful; he will not let you be tempted beyond what you can bear. But when you are tempted, he will also provide a way out so that you can endure it.

Day 52
忍耐必蒙記念
Endurance Will Be Remembered

(1 Thessalonians; Chapter 1: Verse 2-3)

²We always thank God for all of you and continually mention you in our prayers. ³We remember before our God and Father your work produced by faith, your labor prompted by love, and your endurance inspired by hope in our Lord Jesus Christ.

（帖撒羅尼迦前書；1章，2-3節）

²我們為你們眾人常常感謝神，禱告的時候提到你們，³在神我們的父面前，不住的記念你們因信心所做的工夫，因愛心所受的勞苦，因盼望我們主耶穌基督所存的忍耐。

Vocabulary

always [ˈɔlˌwez] adv. 總是
continually [kənˈtɪnjuəli] adv. 持續地
prayer [ˈprɛr] n. 祈禱
produce [prəˈduːs] v. 產生
hope [hop] n. 希望
thank [θæŋk] v. 感謝
mention [ˈmɛnʃən] v. 提及
work [wɝk] n. 工作
faith [feθ] n. 信心

We always thank God for all of you and continually mention you in our prayers. We remember before our God and Father your work produced by faith, your labor prompted by love, and your endurance inspired by hope in our Lord Jesus Christ.

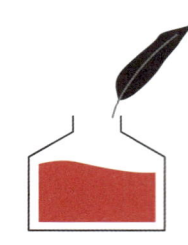

Day 53
忍耐免去試煉
Endurance Keeps from the Trial

(Revelation; Chapter 3: Verse 10-11)

10 Since you have kept my command to endure patiently, I will also keep you from the hour of trial that is going to come on the whole world to test the inhabitants of the earth. **11** I am coming soon. Hold on to what you have, so that no one will take your crown.

（啟示錄；3章，10-11節）

10 你既遵守我忍耐的道，我必在普天下人受試煉的時候，保守你免去你的試煉。**11** 我必快來，你要持守你所有的，免得人奪去你的冠冕。

Vocabulary

command [kəˈmænd] n. 命令	endure [ɪnˈdjʊr] v. 忍耐
patiently [ˈpeɪʃəntlɪ] adv. 耐心地	trial [ˈtraɪəl] n. 試煉
whole [hol] adj. 整個	world [wɝld] n. 世界
test [tɛst] v. 測試	inhabitant [ɪnˈhæbɪtənt] n. 居民
hold on to 保留，保存	crown [kraʊn] 王冠，皇冠

Since you have kept my command to endure patiently, I will also keep you from the hour of trial that is going to come on the whole world to test the inhabitants of the earth. I am coming soon. Hold on to what you have, so that no one will take your crown.

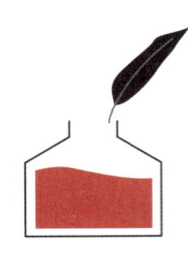

Day 54
忍耐受迫得福
Blessed Are Those Who Are Persecuted

(Matthew; Chapter 5: Verse 10-11)

¹⁰ Blessed are those who are persecuted because of righteousness, for theirs is the kingdom of heaven. ¹¹ "Blessed are you when people insult you, persecute you and falsely say all kinds of evil against you because of me.

（馬太福音；5章，10-11節）

¹⁰ 為義受逼迫的人有福了！因為天國是他們的。¹¹ 人若因我辱罵你們，逼迫你們，捏造各樣壞話毀謗你們，你們就有福了！

Vocabulary

blessed [ˈblɛst] adj. 有福的	persecute [ˈpɜ˞sɪˌkjutɪd] v. 迫害
righteousness [ˈraɪtʃəsnəs] n. 公義	kingdom [ˈkɪŋdəm] n. 王國
heaven [ˈhɛvən] n. 天堂	insult [ˈɪnˌsʌlt] n. 侮辱
evil [ˈivəl] n. 邪惡	

Blessed are those who are persecuted because of righteousness, for theirs is the kingdom of heaven. "Blessed are you when people insult you, persecute you and falsely say all kinds of evil against you because of me.

Day 55
行善受苦忍耐
Suffer for Doing Good

(1 Peter; Chapter 2: Verse 20-21)

20 But how is it to your credit if you receive a beating for doing wrong and endure it? But if you suffer for doing good and you endure it, this is commendable before God. **21** To this you were called, because Christ suffered for you, leaving you an example, that you should follow in his steps.

（彼得前書；2章，20-21節）

20 你們若因犯罪受責打，能忍耐，有什麼可誇的呢？但你們若因行善受苦，能忍耐，這在神看是可喜愛的。**21** 你們蒙召原是為此；因基督也為你們受過苦，給你們留下榜樣，叫你們跟隨祂的腳蹤行。

Vocabulary

credit [ˈkrɛdɪt] **n.** 功勞
wrong [rɔŋ] **adj.** 錯誤的
suffer [ˈsʌfɚ] **v.** 受苦
commendable [kəˈmɛndəbəl] **adj.** 值得讚揚的
before [bɪˈfɔr] **prep.** 在…之前
receive [rɪˈsiv] **v.** 接受
endure [ɪnˈdjʊr] **v.** 忍受
good [gʊd] **adj.** 善良的

But how is it to your credit if you receive a beating for doing wrong and endure it? But if you suffer for doing good and you endure it, this is commendable before God. To this you were called, because Christ suffered for you, leaving you an example, that you should follow in his steps.

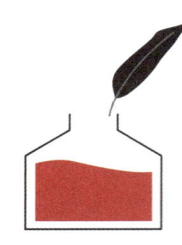

Day 56
患難中要忍耐 Patient in Affliction

(Romans; Chapter 12: Verse 12-14)

12 Be joyful in hope, patient in affliction, faithful in prayer. 13 Share with the Lord's people who are in need. Practice hospitality. 14 Bless those who persecute you; bless and do not curse.

（羅馬書；12章，12-14節）

12 在指望中要喜樂，在患難中要忍耐，禱告要恆切。13 聖徒缺乏要幫補；客要一味的款待。14 逼迫你們的，要給他們祝福；只要祝福，不可咒詛。

Vocabulary

joyful [ˈdʒɔɪfəl] **adj.** 喜樂的	hope [hop] **n.** 希望
patient [ˈpeʃənt] **adj.** 有耐心的	affliction [əˈflɪkʃən] **n.** 苦難
faithful [ˈfeθfəl] **adj.** 忠誠的	prayer [ˈprɛr] **n.** 禱告
share [ʃɛr] **v.** 分享	need [nid] **n.** 需要
people [ˈpipəl] **n.** 人們	

Be joyful in hope, patient in affliction, faithful in prayer. Share with the Lord's people who are in need. Practice hospitality. Bless those who persecute you; bless and do not curse.

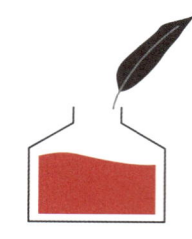

Day 57
歡歡喜喜忍耐
Endurance and Patience with Joy

(Colossians; Chapter 1: Verse 10-11)

¹⁰ so that you may live a life worthy of the Lord and please him in every way: bearing fruit in every good work, growing in the knowledge of God, ¹¹ being strengthened with all power according to his glorious might so that you may have great endurance and patience,

（歌羅西書；1章，10-11節）

¹⁰ 好叫你們行事為人對得起主，凡事蒙祂喜悅，在一切善事上結果子，漸漸的多知道神；¹¹ 照祂榮耀的權能，得以在各樣的力上加力，好叫你們凡事歡歡喜喜的忍耐寬容；

Vocabulary

live [lɪv] v. 活著
worthy [ˈwɝði] adj. 適合…的
bear [ˈbɛr] v. 結出
grow [ˈgro] v. 增多
strengthen [ˈstrɛnθən] 增強，加強
glorious [ˈglorɪəs] adj. 光榮的

life [laɪf] n. 生命
please [pliz] v. 取悅
fruit [frut] n. 果實
knowledge [ˈnɑlɪdʒ] n. 知識
according to 根據…
might [maɪt] n. 力量

so that you may live a life worthy of the Lord and please him in every way: bearing fruit in every good work, growing in the knowledge of God, being strengthened with all power according to his glorious might so that you may have great endurance and patience,

Day 58
忍耐恩典夠用 Grace Is Sufficient

(2 Corinthians; Chapter 12: Verse 9-10)

⁹ But he said to me, "My grace is sufficient for you, for my power is made perfect in weakness." Therefore I will boast all the more gladly about my weaknesses, so that Christ's power may rest on me. ¹⁰ That is why, for Christ's sake, I delight in weaknesses, in insults, in hardships, in persecutions, in difficulties. For when I am weak, then I am strong.

（哥林多後書；12章，9-10節）

⁹ 祂對我說：我的恩典夠你用的，因為我的能力是在人的軟弱上顯得完全。所以，我更喜歡誇自己的軟弱，好叫基督的能力覆庇我。¹⁰ 我為基督的緣故，就以軟弱、凌辱、急難、逼迫、困苦為可喜樂的；因我什麼時候軟弱，什麼時候就剛強了。

Vocabulary

grace [greɪs] n. 恩典
power [ˈpaʊɚ] n. 力量
weakness [ˈwiknəs] n. 軟弱
boast [bost] v. 誇耀
hardships [ˈhardʃɪps] n. 艱難

sufficient [səˈfɪʃənt] adj. 足夠的
perfect [ˈpɝːfɪkt] adj. 完美的
gladly [ˈglædli] adv. 欣然地
delight [dɪˈlaɪt] v. 喜悅
persecution [ˌpɝsɪˈkjuʃən] n. 迫害

But he said to me, "My grace is sufficient for you, for my power is made perfect in weakness." Therefore I will boast all the more gladly about my weaknesses, so that Christ's power may rest on me. That is why, for Christ's sake, I delight in weaknesses, in insults, in hardships, in persecutions, in difficulties. For when I am weak, then I am strong.

Day 59
忍耐望見未來
Endurance Achieves Eternal Glory

(2 Corinthians; Chapter 4: Verse 16-18)

¹⁶ Therefore we do not lose heart. Though outwardly we are wasting away, yet inwardly we are being renewed day by day. ¹⁷ For our light and momentary troubles are achieving for us an eternal glory that far outweighs them all. ¹⁸ So we fix our eyes not on what is seen, but on what is unseen, since what is seen is temporary, but what is unseen is eternal.

（哥林多後書；4章，16-18節）

¹⁶ 所以，我們不喪膽。外體雖然毀壞，內心卻一天新似一天。¹⁷ 我們這至暫至輕的苦楚，要為我們成就極重無比、永遠的榮耀。¹⁸ 原來我們不是顧念所見的，乃是顧念所不見的；因為所見的是暫時的，所不見的是永遠的。

Vocabulary

lose [luz] v. 失去	heart [hɑrt] n. 心
outwardly [ˈaʊtwɚdli] adv. 外在地	waste away 消瘦
renew [rɪˈnu] v. 更新	momentary [ˈmoʊmənˌtɛri] adj. 短暫的
eternal [ɪˈtɝnəl] adj. 永恆的	glory [ˈɡlɔri] n. 榮耀
temporary [ˈtɛmpəˌrɛri] adj. 暫時的	unseen [ʌnˈsin] adj. 看不見的

Therefore we do not lose heart. Though outwardly we are wasting away, yet inwardly we are being renewed day by day. For our light and momentary troubles are achieving for us an eternal glory that far outweighs them all. So we fix our eyes not on what is seen, but on what is unseen, since what is seen is temporary, but what is unseen is eternal.

Day 60
忍耐直到主來
Be Patient until the LORD's Coming

(James; Chapter 5: Verse 7-8)

⁷ Be patient, then, brothers and sisters, until the Lord's coming. See how the farmer waits for the land to yield its valuable crop, patiently waiting for the autumn and spring rains. ⁸ You too, be patient and stand firm, because the Lord's coming is near.

（雅各書；5 章，7-8 節）

⁷ 弟兄們哪，你們要忍耐，直到主來。看哪，農夫忍耐等候地裡寶貴的出產，直到得了秋雨春雨。⁸ 你們也當忍耐，堅固你們的心；因為主來的日子近了。

Vocabulary

patient [ˈpeɪʃənt] **adj.** 耐心的
sister [ˈsɪstɚz] **n.** 姊妹
wait [wet] **v.** 等待
valuable [ˈvæljuəbəl] **adj.** 有價值的
rain [ren] **n.** 雨水

brother [ˈbrʌðɚ] **n.** 兄弟
farmer [ˈfarmɚ] **n.** 農夫
yield [jild] **v.** 生產
autumn [ˈɔtəm] **n.** 秋季

Be patient, then, brothers and sisters, until the Lord's coming. See how the farmer waits for the land to yield its valuable crop, patiently waiting for the autumn and spring rains. You too, be patient and stand firm, because the Lord's coming is near.

自我反思

我們一起完成了忍耐篇 15 天的閱讀與抄寫,現在就透過以下問題來看看各位所獲得的成果。

- 在忍耐篇中,最令您印象深刻的金句是哪一句?

....
....
....
....

- 這 15 天的單元中,您最喜歡哪一天的內容?為什麼?

....
....
....
....

Chapter 5
恩慈

(Psalm 103: Verse 8)

8 The Lord is compassionate and gracious, slow to anger, abounding in love.

（詩篇 103 篇，8 節）

8 耶和華有憐憫，有恩典，不輕易發怒，且有豐盛的慈愛。

Chapter5.mp3

Day 61
神以恩慈救人
Saved by God's Grace

(Ephesians; Chapter 2: Verse 6-8)

⁶ And God raised us up with Christ and seated us with him in the heavenly realms in Christ Jesus, ⁷ in order that in the coming ages he might show the incomparable riches of his grace, expressed in his kindness to us in Christ Jesus. ⁸ For it is by grace you have been saved, through faith—and this is not from yourselves, it is the gift of God

（以弗所書；2 章，6-8 節）

⁶ 祂又叫我們與基督耶穌一同復活、一同坐在天上、⁷ 要將祂極豐富的恩典、就是祂在基督耶穌裏向我們所施的恩慈、顯明給後來的世代看。⁸ 你們得救是本乎恩、也因著信、這並不是出於自己、乃是神所賜的。

Vocabulary

seat [ˈsit] v. 使就座
realm [rɛlm] n. 領域
incomparable [ɪnˈkɑmprəbəl] adj. 無可比擬的
grace [ɡres] n. 恩典
gift [ɡɪft] n. 禮物

heavenly [ˈhɛvənli] adj. 天上的
age [eɪdʒ] n. 年齡
riches [ˈrɪtʃɪz] n. 財富
faith [feθ] n. 信心

And God raised us up with Christ and seated us with him in the heavenly realms in Christ Jesus, in order that in the coming ages he might show the incomparable riches of his grace, expressed in his kindness to us in Christ Jesus. For it is by grace you have been saved, through faith—and this is not from yourselves, it is the gift of God

Day 62
神的恩慈顯明
God's Kindness Appears

(Titus; Chapter 3: Verse 4-5)

⁴ But when the kindness and love of God our Savior appeared, ⁵ he saved us, not because of righteous things we had done, but because of his mercy. He saved us through the washing of rebirth and renewal by the Holy Spirit,

（提多書；3章，4-5節）

⁴ 但到了神我們救主的恩慈、和他向人所施的慈愛顯明的時候、⁵ 他便救了我們、並不是因我們自己所行的義、乃是照他的憐憫、藉著重生的洗、和聖靈的更新。

Vocabulary

kindness [ˈkaɪndnɪs] n. 仁慈
savior [ˈsevjɚ] n. 救世主
righteous [ˈraɪtʃəs] adj. 公義的
washing [ˈwɑʃɪŋ] n. 洗滌
renewal [rɪˈnuəl] n. 更新

love [lʌv] n. 愛
appear [əˈpɪr] v. 出現
mercy [ˈmɝsi] n. 憐憫
rebirth [ˌrɪˈbɝθ] n. 重生

But when the kindness and love of God our Savior appeared, he saved us, not because of righteous things we had done, but because of his mercy. He saved us through the washing of rebirth and renewal by the Holy Spirit,

Day 63
神的恩慈憐憫
God's Mercy and Compassion

(Exodus; Chapter 33: Verse 19)

¹⁹ And the Lord said, "I will cause all my goodness to pass in front of you, and I will proclaim my name, the Lord, in your presence. I will have mercy on whom I will have mercy, and I will have compassion on whom I will have compassion.

（出埃及記；33 章，19 節）

¹⁹ 耶和華說：我要顯我一切的恩慈，在你面前經過，宣告我的名。我要恩待誰就恩待誰；要憐憫誰就憐憫誰；

Vocabulary

cause [kɔz] v. 使發生
proclaim [proʊˈklem] v. 宣告
mercy [ˈmɝsi] n. 憐憫
pass [pæs] v. 經過
presence [ˈprɛzəns] n. 存在，出現
compassion [kəmˈpæʃən] n. 同情

And the Lord said, "I will cause all my goodness to pass in front of you, and I will proclaim my name, the Lord, in your presence. I will have mercy on whom I will have mercy, and I will have compassion on whom I will have compassion.

Day 64

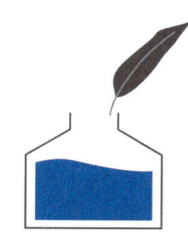

神的恩慈照顧
No One Is Cast off by the LORD

(Lamentations; Chapter 3: Verse 31-33)

31 For no one is cast off by the Lord forever. **32** Though he brings grief, he will show compassion, so great is his unfailing love. **33** For he does not willingly bring affliction or grief to anyone.

（耶利米哀歌；3 章，31-33 節）

31 因為主必不永遠丟棄人。**32** 主雖使人憂愁，還要照祂諸般的慈愛發憐憫。**33** 因祂並不甘心使人受苦，使人憂愁。

Vocabulary

cast off [kæst ɔf] v. 拋棄
bring [brɪŋ] v. 帶來
show [ʃo] v. 顯示
love [lʌv] n. 愛
willingly [ˈwɪlɪŋlɪ] adv. 自願地

forever [fəˈrɛvər] adv. 永遠
grief [grif] n. 悲痛
unfailing [ʌnˈfelɪŋ] adj. 經久不衰的，一貫的
affliction [əˈflɪkʃən] n. 苦難

For no one is cast off by the Lord forever. Though he brings grief, he will show compassion, so great is his unfailing love. For he does not willingly bring affliction or grief to anyone.

Day 65
神的恩慈堅定 God's Unfailing Love

(Isaiah; Chapter 54: Verse 10-11)

10 Though the mountains be shaken and the hills be removed, yet my unfailing love for you will not be shaken nor my covenant of peace be removed," says the Lord, who has compassion on you. **11** "Afflicted city, lashed by storms and not comforted, I will rebuild you with stones of turquoise, your foundations with lapis lazuli.

（以賽亞書；54 章，10-11 節）

10 大山可以挪開，小山可以遷移；但我的慈愛必不離開你；我平安的約也不遷移。這是憐恤你的耶和華說的。**11** 你這受困苦、被風飄蕩不得安慰的人哪，我必以彩色安置你的石頭，以藍寶石立定你的根基；

Vocabulary

mountain [ˈmaʊntɪn] n. 山	shake [ˈʃek] v. 搖動，震動
hill [hɪl] n. 山丘	remove [rɪˈmuv] v. 移除
covenant [ˈkʌvənənt] n. 盟約	peace [pis] n. 和平
compassion [kəmˈpæʃən] n. 憐憫	afflicted [əˈflɪktɪd] adj. 受苦的
rebuild [rɪˈbɪld] v. 重建	stone [ston] n. 石頭

Though the mountains be shaken and the hills be removed, yet my unfailing love for you will not be shaken nor my covenant of peace be removed," says the Lord, who has compassion on you. "Afflicted city, lashed by storms and not comforted, I will rebuild you with stones of turquoise, your foundations with lapis lazuli.

Day 66

神的恩慈要求
The Mercy God Requires

(Micah; Chapter 6: Verse 7-8)

⁷ Will the Lord be pleased with thousands of rams, with ten thousand rivers of olive oil? Shall I offer my firstborn for my transgression, the fruit of my body for the sin of my soul? ⁸ He has shown you, O mortal, what is good. And what does the Lord require of you? To act justly and to love mercy and to walk humbly with your God.

（彌迦書；6章，7-8節）

⁷ 耶和華豈喜悅千千的公羊，或是萬萬的油河嗎？我豈可為自己的罪過獻我的長子嗎？為心中的罪惡獻我身所生的嗎？⁸ 世人哪，耶和華已指示你何為善。祂向你所要的是什麼呢？只要你行公義，好憐憫，存謙卑的心，與你的神同行。

Vocabulary

ram [ræm] n. 公羊
firstborn [ˈfɚstˌbɔrn] n. 長子
sin [sɪn] n. 罪
require [rɪˈkwaɪr] v. 要求
justly [ˈdʒʌstlɪ] adv. 公正地
walk [wɔk] v. 行走

offer [ˈɔːfɚ] v. 獻上
transgression [trænsˈɡrɛʃən] n. 罪惡
mortal [ˈmɔrtəl] n. 凡人
act [ækt] v. 行動
mercy [ˈmɝsɪ] n. 憐憫
humbly [ˈhʌmblɪ] adv. 謙卑地

Will the Lord be pleased with thousands of rams, with ten thousand rivers of olive oil? Shall I offer my firstborn for my transgression, the fruit of my body for the sin of my soul? He has shown you, O mortal, what is good. And what does the Lord require of you? To act justly and to love mercy and to walk humbly with your God.

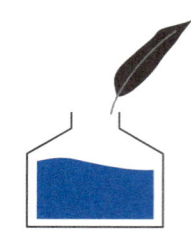

Day 67
選民恩慈存心
The Kindness of God's Chosen Ones

(Colossians; Chapter 3: Verse 12-13)

¹² Therefore, as God's chosen people, holy and dearly loved, clothe yourselves with compassion, kindness, humility, gentleness and patience. ¹³ Bear with each other and forgive one another if any of you has a grievance against someone. Forgive as the Lord forgave you.

（歌羅西書；3章，12-13節）

¹² 所以，你們既是神的選民，聖潔蒙愛的人，就要存（原文作穿；下同）憐憫、恩慈、謙虛、溫柔、忍耐的心。¹³ 倘若這人與那人有嫌隙，總要彼此包容，彼此饒恕；主怎樣饒恕了你們，你們也要怎樣饒恕人。

Vocabulary

chosen [ˈtʃozən] **adj.** 被選的
clothe [kloð] **v.** 使穿上
gentleness [ˈdʒɛntlnəs] **n.** 溫和
forgive [fɚˈgɪv] **v.** 寬恕
bear [bɛr] **v.** 忍受

loved [lʌvd] **adj.** 被愛的
humility [hjuˈmɪləti] **n.** 謙遜
patience [ˈpeɪʃəns] **n.** 耐心
grievance [ˈgrivəns] **n.** 不滿

Therefore, as God's chosen people, holy and dearly loved, clothe yourselves with compassion, kindness, humility, gentleness and patience. Bear with each other and forgive one another if any of you has a grievance against someone. Forgive as the Lord forgave you.

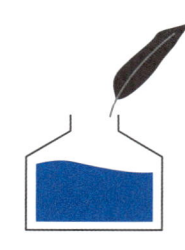

Day 68
要以恩慈相待
Be Kind to One Another

(Ephesians; Chapter 4: Verse 31-32)

³¹ Get rid of all bitterness, rage and anger, brawling and slander, along with every form of malice. ³² Be kind and compassionate to one another, forgiving each other, just as in Christ God forgave you.

（以弗所書；4 章，31-32 節）

³¹ 一切苦毒、惱恨、忿怒、嚷鬧、毀謗，並一切的惡毒（或作：陰毒），都當從你們中間除掉；³² 並要以恩慈相待，存憐憫的心，彼此饒恕，正如神在基督裡饒恕了你們一樣。

Vocabulary

bitterness [ˈbɪtɚnəs] n. 苦澀
anger [ˈæŋɚ] n. 憤怒
slander [ˈslændɚ] n. 誹謗
kind [kaɪnd] adj. 仁慈的
forgive [fɚˈgɪv] v. 寬恕

rage [redʒ] n. 憤怒
brawling [ˈbrɔˌlɪŋ] n. 爭吵
malice [ˈmæləs] n. 惡意
compassion [kəmˈpæʃən] n. 憐憫

Get rid of all bitterness, rage and anger, brawling and slander, along with every form of malice. Be kind and compassionate to one another, forgiving each other, just as in Christ God forgave you.

Day 69
正直人有恩慈
Upright People are Gracious

(Psalm 112: Verse 4-6)

⁴ Even in darkness light dawns for the upright, for those who are gracious and compassionate and righteous. ⁵ Good will come to those who are generous and lend freely, who conduct their affairs with justice. ⁶ Surely the righteous will never be shaken; they will be remembered forever.

（詩篇 112 篇，4-6 節）

⁴ 正直人在黑暗中，有光向他發現；他有恩惠，有憐憫，有公義。⁵ 施恩與人、借貸與人的，這人事情順利；他被審判的時候要訴明自己的冤。⁶ 他永不動搖；義人被記念，直到永遠。

Vocabulary

darkness [ˈdɑrkˌnəs] **n.** 黑暗	light [laɪt] **n.** 光
dawn [dɔn] **v.** 破曉	upright [ˈʌpraɪt] **adj.** 正直的
gracious [ˈgreɪʃəs] **adj.** 親切的	compassionate [kəmˈpæʃənət] **adj.** 有同情心的
righteous [ˈraɪtʃəs] **adj.** 正義的	generous [ˈdʒɛnərəs] **adj.** 慷慨的
justice [ˈdʒʌstɪs] **n.** 公義	

Even in darkness light dawns for the upright, for those who are gracious and compassionate and righteous. Good will come to those who are generous and lend freely, who conduct their affairs with justice. Surely the righteous will never be shaken; they will be remembered forever.

Day 70

恩慈必得豐裕
Generous Person Will Prosper

(Proverbs; Chapter 11: Verse 24-26)

24 One person gives freely, yet gains even more; another withholds unduly, but comes to poverty. **25** A generous person will prosper; whoever refreshes others will be refreshed. **26** People curse the one who hoards grain, but they pray God's blessing on the one who is willing to sell.

（箴言；11 章，24-26 節）

24 有施散的，卻更增添；有吝惜過度的，反致窮乏。**25** 好施捨的，必得豐裕；滋潤人的，必得滋潤。**26** 屯糧不賣的，民必咒詛他；情願出賣的，人必為他祝福。

Vocabulary

freely [ˈfriːlɪ] **adv.** 自由地
withhold [wɪðˈhoʊld] **v.** 保留
poverty [ˈpɑvɚtɪ] **n.** 貧困
prosper [ˈprɑspɚ] **v.** 繁榮
hoard [hord] **v.** 貯藏

gain [gen] **v.** 獲得
unduly [ʌnˈduːlɪ] **adv.** 過度地
generous [ˈdʒɛnərəs] **adj.** 慷慨的
refresh [rɪˈfrɛʃ] **v.** 使恢復活力

One person gives freely, yet gains even more; another withholds unduly, but comes to poverty. A generous person will prosper; whoever refreshes others will be refreshed. People curse the one who hoards grain, but they pray God's blessing on the one who is willing to sell.

Day 71
恩慈多行善事
Generous on Every Occasion

(2 Corinthians; Chapter 9: Verse 9-11)

⁹ As it is written: "They have freely scattered their gifts to the poor; their righteousness endures forever." ¹⁰ Now he who supplies seed to the sower and bread for food will also supply and increase your store of seed and will enlarge the harvest of your righteousness. ¹¹ You will be enriched in every way so that you can be generous on every occasion, and through us your generosity will result in thanksgiving to God.

（哥林多後書；9 章，9-11 節）

⁹ 如經上所記：他施捨錢財，賙濟貧窮；他的仁義存到永遠。 ¹⁰ 那賜種給撒種的，賜糧給人吃的，必多多加給你們種地的種子，又增添你們仁義的果子； ¹¹ 叫你們凡事富足，可以多多施捨，就藉著我們使感謝歸於神。

Vocabulary

- scatter [ˈskætɚ] **v.** 散布
- poor [pʊr] **adj.** 貧窮的
- endure [ɪnˈdjʊr] **v.** 持續
- increase [ɪnˈkris] **v.** 增加
- enriched [ɪnˈrɪtʃt] **adj.** 富足的
- gift [gɪft] **n.** 禮物
- righteousness [ˈraɪtʃəsnəs] **n.** 公義
- supply [səˈplaɪ] **v.** 供應
- enlarge [ɪnˈlardʒ] **v.** 擴大

As it is written: "They have freely scattered their gifts to the poor; their righteousness endures forever." Now he who supplies seed to the sower and bread for food will also supply and increase your store of seed and will enlarge the harvest of your righteousness. You will be enriched in every way so that you can be generous on every occasion, and through us your generosity will result in thanksgiving to God.

Day 72

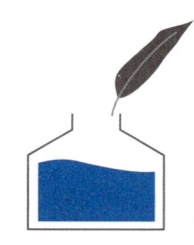

恩慈牧養群羊
Care God's Flock with Willing

(1 Peter; Chapter 5: Verse 2-3)

² Be shepherds of God's flock that is under your care, watching over them—not because you must, but because you are willing, as God wants you to be; not pursuing dishonest gain, but eager to serve; ³ not lording it over those entrusted to you, but being examples to the flock.

（彼得前書；5 章，2-3 節）

² 務要牧養在你們中間神的群羊，按著神旨意照管他們；不是出於勉強，乃是出於甘心；也不是因為貪財，乃是出於樂意；³ 也不是轄制所託付你們的，乃是作群羊的榜樣。

Vocabulary

shepherd [ˈʃɛpərd] **n.** 牧者
willing [ˈwɪlɪŋ] **adj.** 願意的
gain [geɪn] **n.** 獲得，獲利
lord it over... 對（某人）發號施令
example [ɪɡˈzæmpəl] **n.** 榜樣

flock [flɑk] **n.** 羊群（或群體）
dishonest [dɪsˈɑnəst] **adj.** 不誠實的
serve [sɝv] **v.** 供應，服務
entrust [ɪnˈtrʌst] **v.** 委託

Be shepherds of God's flock that is under your care, watching over them—not because you must, but because you are willing, as God wants you to be; not pursuing dishonest gain, but eager to serve; not lording it over those entrusted to you, but being examples to the flock.

Day 73

恩慈絕不被棄
Never the Righteous Be Forsaken

(Psalm 37: Verse 25-27)

²⁵ I was young and now I am old, yet I have never seen the righteous forsaken or their children begging bread. ²⁶ They are always generous and lend freely; their children will be a blessing. ²⁷ Turn from evil and do good; then you will dwell in the land forever.

（詩篇 37 篇，25-27 節）

²⁵ 我從前年幼，現在年老，卻未見過義人被棄，也未見過他的後裔討飯。²⁶ 他終日恩待人，借給人；他的後裔也蒙福！²⁷ 你當離惡行善，就可永遠安居。

Vocabulary

young [jʌŋ] adj. 年輕的	old [old] adj. 老的
righteous [ˈraɪtʃəs] adj. 正義的	forsaken [fɚˈsekən] 被遺棄的
beg [ˈbɛg] v. 乞求	generous [ˈdʒɛnərəs] adj. 慷慨的
lend [lɛnd] v. 借出	blessing [ˈblɛsɪŋ] n. 祝福
turn [tɝn] v. 轉向	dwell [dwɛl] v. 居住

I was young and now I am old, yet I have never seen the righteous forsaken or their children begging bread. They are always generous and lend freely; their children will be a blessing. Turn from evil and do good; then you will dwell in the land forever.

Day 74
恩慈適應眾人
Share Blessings with Everyone

(1 Corinthians; Chapter 9: Verse 22-23)

²² To the weak I became weak, to win the weak. I have become all things to all people so that by all possible means I might save some. ²³ I do all this for the sake of the gospel, that I may share in its blessings.

（哥林多前書；9 章，22-23 節）

²² 向軟弱的人，我就作軟弱的人，為要得軟弱的人。向什麼樣的人，我就作什麼樣的人。無論如何，總要救些人。²³ 凡我所行的，都是為福音的緣故，為要與人同得這福音的好處。

Vocabulary

weak [wik] **adj.** 弱的
things [θɪŋz] **n.** 事物
possible [ˈpɑsəbəl] **adj.** 可能的
save [seɪv] **v.** 拯救
blessings [ˈblɛsɪŋz] **n.** 祝福

all [ɔl] **adj.** 全部的
people [ˈpipəl] **n.** 人們
means [minz] **n.** 方法
gospel [ˈɡɑspəl] **n.** 福音

To the weak I became weak, to win the weak. I have become all things to all people so that by all possible means I might save some. I do all this for the sake of the gospel, that I may share in its blessings.

Day 75
恩慈嚴厲有別
God's Kindness and Sternness

(Romans; Chapter 11: Verse 22)

22 Consider therefore the kindness and sternness of God: sternness to those who fell, but kindness to you, provided that you continue in his kindness. Otherwise, you also will be cut off.

（羅馬書；11章，22節）

22 可見神的恩慈和嚴厲，向那跌倒的人是嚴厲的，向你是有恩慈的；只要你長久在祂的恩慈裡，不然，你也要被砍下來。

Vocabulary

consider [kənˈsɪdər] v. 考慮
kindness [ˈkaɪndnəs] n. 仁慈
continue [kənˈtɪnˌju] v. 繼續
cut off 斷絕

therefore [ˈðɛrfɔr] adv. 因此
sternness [ˈstɜ˞nˌnəs] n. 嚴厲
provided [prəˈvaɪdɪd] 假如
otherwise [ˈʌðɚˌwaɪz] adv. 否則

Consider therefore the kindness and sternness of God: sternness to those who fell, but kindness to you, provided that you continue in his kindness. Otherwise, you also will be cut off.

自我反思

我們一起完成了恩慈篇 15 天的閱讀與抄寫,現在就透過以下問題來看看各位所獲得的成果。

- 在恩慈篇中,最令您印象深刻的金句是哪一句?

- 這 15 天的單元中,您最喜歡哪一天的內容?為什麼?

Chapter 6
良善

(Romans; Chapter 15: Verse 14)

14 I myself am convinced, my brothers and sisters, that you yourselves are full of goodness, filled with knowledge and competent to instruct one another.

（羅馬書；15章，14節）

14 弟兄們，我自己也深信你們是滿有良善，充足了諸般的知識，也能彼此勸戒。

Chapter6.mp3

Day 76
耶和華本為善 The LORD Is Good

(Psalm 107: Verse 1-3)

¹ Give thanks to the Lord, for he is good; his love endures forever. ² Let the redeemed of the Lord tell their story— those he redeemed from the hand of the foe, ³ those he gathered from the lands, from east and west, from north and south.

（詩篇；107 篇，1-3 節）

¹ 你們要稱謝耶和華，因祂本為善；祂的慈愛永遠長存！² 願耶和華的贖民說這話，就是祂從敵人手中所救贖的，³ 從各地，從東從西，從南從北，所招聚來的。

Vocabulary

- love [lʌv] n. 愛
- redeemed [rɪˈdimd] adj. 被拯救的
- foe [fo] n. 敵人
- land [lænd] n. 土地
- endure [ɪnˈdʊr] v. 持續
- story [ˈstɔrɪ] n. 故事
- gather [ˈgæðɚ] v. 聚集

Give thanks to the Lord, for he is good; his love endures forever. Let the redeemed of the Lord tell their story— those he redeemed from the hand of the foe, those he gathered from the lands, from east and west, from north and south.

Day 77
察驗神的善良
Test and Approve God's Will

(Romans; Chapter 12: Verse 2)

² Do not conform to the pattern of this world, but be transformed by the renewing of your mind. Then you will be able to test and approve what God's will is—his good, pleasing and perfect will.

（羅馬書；12章，2節）

² 不要效法這個世界，只要心意更新而變化，叫你們察驗何為神的善良、純全、可喜悅的旨意。

Vocabulary

conform to 遵從
world [wɝld] n. 世界
mind [maɪnd] n. 心；想法
approve [əˈpruv] v. 批准
perfect [ˈpɝːfɪkt] adj. 完美的

pattern [ˈpætɚn] n. 模式
transform [trænsˈfɔrm] v. 改變
test [tɛst] v. 測試，檢驗
pleasing [ˈplizɪŋ] adj. 令人愉快的

Do not conform to the pattern of this world, but be transformed by the renewing of your mind. Then you will be able to test and approve what God's will is—his good, pleasing and perfect will.

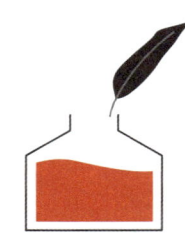

Day 78
聖潔以備行善
Cleanse Ourselves for Doing Good Work

(2 Timothy; Chapter 2: Verse 21)

²¹ Those who cleanse themselves from the latter will be instruments for special purposes, made holy, useful to the Master and prepared to do any good work.

（提摩太後書；2 章，21 節）

²¹ 人若自潔，脫離卑賤的事，就必作貴重的器皿，成為聖潔，合乎主用，預備行各樣的善事。

Vocabulary

cleanse [klɛnz] v. 清潔
special [ˈspɛʃəl] adj. 特別的
holy [ˈholɪ] adj. 聖潔的
prepared [prɪˈpɛrd] adj. 準備好的

instrument [ˈɪnstrəmənt] n. 工具
purpose [ˈpɝpəs] n. 目的
useful [ˈjusfəl] adj. 有用的

Those who cleanse themselves from the latter will be instruments for special purposes, made holy, useful to the Master and prepared to do any good work.

Day 79
聖經教導行善
Bible Teaches Good Work

(2 Timothy; Chapter 3: Verse 16-17)

¹⁶ All Scripture is God-breathed and is useful for teaching, rebuking, correcting and training in righteousness, ¹⁷ so that the servant of God may be thoroughly equipped for every good work.

（提摩太後書；3章，16-17節）

¹⁶ 聖經都是神所默示的（或作：凡神所默示的聖經），於教訓、督責、使人歸正、教導人學義都是有益的，¹⁷ 叫屬神的人得以完全，預備行各樣的善事。

Vocabulary

Scripture [ˈskrɪptʃɚ] n. 聖經	God-breathed [ɡɑdˈbriθɪd] adj. 神所啟示的
useful [ˈjusfəl] adj. 有用的	teaching [ˈtitʃɪŋ] n. 教學
rebuking [rɪˈbʊkɪŋ] n. 指責	correcting [kəˈrɛktɪŋ] n. 改正
training [ˈtrenɪŋ] n. 訓練	righteousness [ˈraɪtʃəsnəs] n. 正義，公正
servant [ˈsɝvənt] n. 僕人	equipped [ɪˈkwɪpt] adj. 裝備好的

All Scripture is God-breathed and is useful for teaching, rebuking, correcting and training in righteousness, so that the servant of God may be thoroughly equipped for every good work.

Day 80

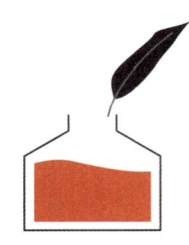

不可以惡報惡
Nobody Pays Back Wrong for Wrong

(1 Thessalonians; Chapter 5: Verse 15)

¹⁵ Make sure that nobody pays back wrong for wrong, but always strive to do what is good for each other and for everyone else.

（帖撒羅尼迦前書；5 章，15 節）

¹⁵ 你們要謹慎，無論是誰都不可以惡報惡；或是彼此相待，或是待眾人，常要追求良善。

Vocabulary

pay back 使付出代價
each other 互相
else [ɛls] adv. 其他

strive [straɪv] v. 努力
everyone [ˈɛvrɪˌwʌn] pron. 每個人
nobody [ˈnoˌbɑdɪ] pron. 沒有人

Make sure that nobody pays back wrong for wrong, but always strive to do what is good for each other and for everyone else.

Day 81
不可忘記行善
Don't Forget to Do Good

(Hebrews; Chapter 13: Verse 15-16)

¹⁵ Through Jesus, therefore, let us continually offer to God a sacrifice of praise—the fruit of lips that openly profess his name. ¹⁶ And do not forget to do good and to share with others, for with such sacrifices God is pleased.

（希伯來書；13 章，15-16 節）

¹⁵ 我們應當靠著耶穌，常常以頌讚為祭獻給神，這就是那承認主名之人嘴唇的果子。¹⁶ 只是不可忘記行善和捐輸的事；因為這樣的祭，是神所喜悅的。

Vocabulary

continually [kənˋtɪnjʊəlɪ] adv. 持續地	offer [ˋɔfɚ] v. 提供
sacrifice [ˋsækrəˌfaɪs] n. 祭品	praise [prez] n. 讚美
fruit [frut] n. 果子	lips [lɪps] n. 嘴唇
openly [ˋopənlɪ] adv. 公開地	profess [prəˋfɛs] v. 宣稱
share [ʃɛr] v. 分享	pleased [plizd] adj. 高興的

Through Jesus, therefore, let us continually offer to God a sacrifice of praise—the fruit of lips that openly profess his name. And do not forget to do good and to share with others, for with such sacrifices God is pleased.

Day 82
行善不可推辭
Don't Withhold from Doing Good

(Proverbs; Chapter 3: Verse 27-29)

²⁷ Do not withhold good from those to whom it is due, when it is in your power to act. ²⁸ Do not say to your neighbor, "Come back tomorrow and I'll give it to you"— when you already have it with you. ²⁹ Do not plot harm against your neighbor, who lives trustfully near you.

（箴言；3章，27-29節）

²⁷ 你手若有行善的力量、不可推辭、就當向那應得的人施行。²⁸ 你那裏若有現成的、不可對鄰舍說、去罷、明天再來、我必給你。²⁹ 你的鄰舍、既在你附近安居、你不可設計害他。

Vocabulary

withhold [wɪðˈhoʊld] v. 保留，不給	due [dju] adj. 應有的
power [ˈpaʊɚ] n. 力量	act [ækt] v. 行動
neighbor [ˈnebɚ] n. 鄰居	tomorrow [təˈmaro] adv. 明天
give [gɪv] v. 給予	plot [plɑt] v. 策劃
harm [hɑrm] n. 傷害	trustfully [ˈtrʌstfəlɪ] adv. 信任地

Do not withhold good from those to whom it is due, when it is in your power to act. Do not say to your neighbor, "Come back tomorrow and I'll give it to you"— when you already have it with you. Do not plot harm against your neighbor, who lives trustfully near you.

Day 83

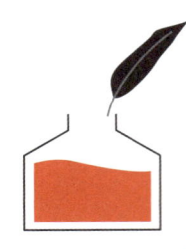

行善不可喪志
Don't Become Weary in Doing Good

(Galatians; Chapter 6: Verse 9-10)

⁹ Let us not become weary in doing good, for at the proper time we will reap a harvest if we do not give up. ¹⁰ Therefore, as we have opportunity, let us do good to all people, especially to those who belong to the family of believers.

（加拉太書；6章，9-10節）

⁹ 我們行善，不可喪志；若不灰心，到了時候就要收成。¹⁰ 所以，有了機會就當向眾人行善，向信徒一家的人更當這樣。

Vocabulary

- weary [ˈwɪrɪ] **adj.** 疲倦的
- harvest [ˈhɑrvɪst] **n.** 收成
- opportunity [ˌɑpəˈtuːnɪtɪ] **n.** 機會
- family [ˈfæməlɪ] **n.** 家庭
- reap [rip] **v.** 收穫
- give up 放棄
- belong to 屬於
- believer [bɪˈlivə] **n.** 信徒

Let us not become weary in doing good, for at the proper time we will reap a harvest if we do not give up. Therefore, as we have opportunity, let us do good to all people, especially to those who belong to the family of believers.

Day 84

行善不求回報
Do Good without Expecting Repayment

(Luke; Chapter 14: Verse 13-14)

¹³ But when you give a banquet, invite the poor, the crippled, the lame, the blind, ¹⁴ and you will be blessed. Although they cannot repay you, you will be repaid at the resurrection of the righteous.

（路加福音；14 章，13-14 節）

¹³ 你擺設筵席，倒要請那貧窮的、殘廢的、瘸腿的、瞎眼的，你就有福了！¹⁴ 因為他們沒有什麼可報答你。到義人復活的時候，你要得著報答。

Vocabulary

banquet [ˈbæŋkwɪt] n. 宴會
poor [pʊr] adj. 貧窮的
lame [lem] adj. 瘸的
blessed [ˈblɛst] adj. 有福的
resurrection [ˌrɛzəˈrɛkʃən] n. 復活

invite [ɪnˈvaɪt] v. 邀請
crippled [ˈkrɪpld] adj. 瘸的／跛的
blind [blaɪnd] adj. 失明的
repay [rɪˈpe] v. 償還
righteous [ˈraɪtʃəs] adj. 正義的

But when you give a banquet, invite the poor, the crippled, the lame, the blind, and you will be blessed. Although they cannot repay you, you will be repaid at the resurrection of the righteous.

Day 85
行善如神有光
Shine Your Light on People in Need

(Isaiah; Chapter 58: Verse 10-11)

¹⁰ and if you spend yourselves in behalf of the hungry and satisfy the needs of the oppressed, then your light will rise in the darkness, and your night will become like the noonday. ¹¹ The Lord will guide you always; he will satisfy your needs in a sun-scorched land and will strengthen your frame. You will be like a well-watered garden, like a spring whose waters never fail.

（以賽亞書；58 章，10-11 節）

¹⁰ 你心若向飢餓的人發憐憫，使困苦的人得滿足，你的光就必在黑暗中發現；你的幽暗必變如正午。¹¹ 耶和華也必時常引導你，在乾旱之地使你心滿意足，骨頭強壯。你必像澆灌的園子，又像水流不絕的泉源。

Vocabulary

spend [spɛnd] v. 花費	hungry [ˈhʌŋgrɪ] adj. 飢餓的
satisfy [ˈsætɪsfaɪ] v. 滿足	oppressed [əˈprɛst] adj. 被壓迫的
light [laɪt] n. 光	darkness [ˈdɑrknəs] n. 黑暗
noonday [ˈnundeɪ] n. 正午	guide [gaɪd] v. 指導
scorched [skɔːtʃt] adj. 燒焦的	strengthen [ˈstrɛŋθən] v. 加強
frame [frem] n. 骨架	garden [ˈgɑrdən] n. 花園

and if you spend yourselves in behalf of the hungry and satisfy the needs of the oppressed, then your light will rise in the darkness, and your night will become like the noonday. The Lord will guide you always; he will satisfy your needs in a sun-scorched land and will strengthen your frame. You will be like a well-watered garden, like a spring whose waters never fail.

Day 86
行善就要大方
Be Generous When Doing Good

(Luke; Chapter 6: Verse 38)

[38] Give, and it will be given to you. A good measure, pressed down, shaken together and running over, will be poured into your lap. For with the measure you use, it will be measured to you.

（路加福音；6 章，38 節）

[38] 你們要給人，就必有給你們的，並且用十足的升斗，連搖帶按，上尖下流的倒在你們懷裡；因為你們用什麼量器量給人，也必用什麼量器量給你們。

Vocabulary

press [prɛs] v. 壓

run [ˈrʌn] v. 流動

use [juz] v. 使用

shake [ˈʃek] v. 搖動

pour [pɔr] v. 倒（出）

measure [ˈmɛʒɚ] v. 衡量

Give, and it will be given to you. A good measure, pressed down, shaken together and running over, will be poured into your lap. For with the measure you use, it will be measured to you.

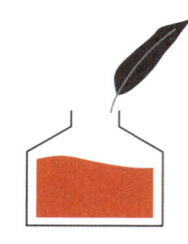

Day 87
求善者得恩惠
Whoever Seeks Good Finds Favor

(Proverbs; Chapter 11: Verse 27-29)

27 Whoever seeks good finds favor, but evil comes to one who searches for it. **28** Those who trust in their riches will fall, but the righteous will thrive like a green leaf. **29** Whoever brings ruin on their family will inherit only wind, and the fool will be servant to the wise.

（箴言；11 章，27-29 節）

27 懇切求善的，就求得恩惠；惟獨求惡的，惡必臨到他身。**28** 倚仗自己財物的，必跌倒；義人必發旺，如青葉。**29** 擾害己家的，必承受清風；愚昧人必作慧心人的僕人。

Vocabulary

seek [sik] v. 尋求
evil [ˈivəl] n. 邪惡
trust [trʌst] v. 信任
fall [fɔl] v. 倒下
leaf [lif] n. 葉子
inherit [ɪnˈhɛrɪt] v. 繼承

favor [ˈfevɚ] n. 好感，恩寵
search [sɝtʃ] v. 搜尋
riches [ˈrɪtʃɪz] n. 財富
thrive [θraɪv] v. 興旺
ruin [ˈruːɪn] n. 毀壞，破壞

Whoever seeks good finds favor, but evil comes to one who searches for it. Those who trust in their riches will fall, but the righteous will thrive like a green leaf. Whoever brings ruin on their family will inherit only wind, and the fool will be servant to the wise.

Day 88

依善行得賞賜
Get Rewards for Good Deeds

(Ephesians; Chapter 6: Verse 7-8)

7 Serve wholeheartedly, as if you were serving the Lord, not people, 8 because you know that the Lord will reward each one for whatever good they do, whether they are slave or free.

（以弗所書；6章，7-8節）

7 甘心事奉，好像服事主，不像服事人。8 因為曉得各人所行的善事，不論是為奴的，是自主的，都必按所行的得主的賞賜。

Vocabulary

wholeheartedly [ˌhol`hartɪdlɪ] adv. 全心全意地

each one 每個人

free [fri] adj. 自由的

reward [rɪ`wɔrd] v. 獎勵

slave [slev] n. 奴隸

Serve wholeheartedly, as if you were serving the Lord, not people, because you know that the Lord will reward each one for whatever good they do, whether they are slave or free.

Day 89
持守善美的事
Hold on to What Is Good

(1 Thessalonians; Chapter 5: Verse 19-22)

¹⁹ Do not quench the Spirit. ²⁰ Do not treat prophecies with contempt ²¹ but test them all; hold on to what is good, ²² reject every kind of evil.

（帖撒羅尼迦前書；5 章，19-22 節）

¹⁹ 不要消滅聖靈的感動；²⁰ 不要藐視先知的講論。²¹ 但要凡事察驗，善美的要持守，²² 各樣的惡事要禁戒不做。

Vocabulary

quench [kwɛntʃ] v. 熄滅
prophecy [ˈprɑfɪsi] n. 預言
test [tɛst] v. 試驗
reject [rɪˈdʒɛkt] v. 拒絕
kind [kaɪnd] n. 種類
treat [trit] v. 對待
contempt [kənˈtɛmpt] n. 輕蔑
hold on 堅持
every [ˈɛvri] adj. 每個

Do not quench the Spirit. Do not treat prophecies with contempt but test them all; hold on to what is good, reject every kind of evil.

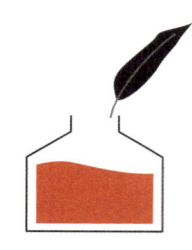

Day 90
富人更該行善
Rich People Should Do Good Deeds

(1 Timothy; Chapter 6: Verse 17-18)

17 Command those who are rich in this present world not to be arrogant nor to put their hope in wealth, which is so uncertain, but to put their hope in God, who richly provides us with everything for our enjoyment. **18** Command them to do good, to be rich in good deeds, and to be generous and willing to share.

（提摩太前書；6 章，17-18 節）

17 你要囑咐那些今世富足的人，不要自高，也不要倚靠無定的錢財；只要倚靠那厚賜百物給我們享受的神。**18** 又要囑咐他們行善，在好事上富足，甘心施捨，樂意供給（或作：體貼）人，

Vocabulary

command [kəˈmænd] v. 命令
present [ˈprɛzənt] adj. 現在的
hope [hop] n. 希望
uncertain [ʌnˈsɝtn] adj. 不確定的
generous [ˈdʒɛnərəs] adj. 慷慨的
deed [diːd] n. 行為

rich [rɪtʃ] adj. 富有的
arrogant [ˈærəgənt] adj. 傲慢的
wealth [wɛlθ] n. 財富
provide [prəˈvaɪd] v. 提供
enjoyment [ɪnˈdʒɔɪmənt] n. 享受
share [ʃɛr] v. 分享

Command those who are rich in this present world not to be arrogant nor to put their hope in wealth, which is so uncertain, but to put their hope in God, who richly provides us with everything for our enjoyment. Command them to do good, to be rich in good deeds, and to be generous and willing to share.

自我反思

我們一起完成了良善篇 15 天的閱讀與抄寫,現在就透過以下問題來看看各位所獲得的成果。

- 在良善篇中,最令您印象深刻的金句是哪一句?

- 這 15 天的單元中,您最喜歡哪一天的內容?為什麼?

Chapter 7
信實

(Proverbs; Chapter 19: Verse 5)

[5] A false witness will not go unpunished, and whoever pours out lies will not go free.

（箴言；19章，5節）

[5] 作假見證的，必不免受罰；吐出謊言的，終不能逃脫。

Chapter7.mp3

Day 91

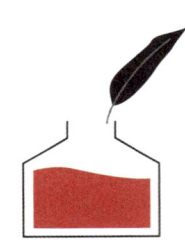

信實神施慈愛
Faithful God Keeping His Covenant of Love

(Deuteronomy; Chapter 7: Verse 9)

⁹Know therefore that the Lord your God is God; he is the faithful God, keeping his covenant of love to a thousand generations of those who love him and keep his commandments.

（申命記；7章，9節）

⁹所以，你要知道耶和華—你的神，他是神，是信實的神；向愛他、守他誡命的人守約，施慈愛，直到千代；

Vocabulary

know [no] **v.** 知道	therefore [ˈðɛrfɔr] **adv.** 因此
faithful [ˈfeθfəl] **adj.** 忠誠的	covenant [ˈkʌvənənt] **n.** 盟約
love [lʌv] **n.** 愛	thousand [ˈθaʊzənd] **adj.** 千
generation [ˌdʒɛnəˈreɪʃən] **n.** 世代	commandment [kəˈmændmənt] **n.** 誡命
keep [ˈkip] **v.** 維持	

Know therefore that the Lord your God is God; he is the faithful God, keeping his covenant of love to a thousand generations of those who love him and keep his commandments.

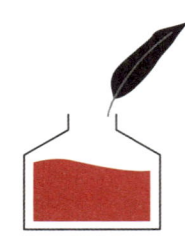

Day 92
信實的神可信 God Remains Faithful

(2 Timothy; Chapter 2: Verse 11-13)

¹¹ Here is a trustworthy saying: If we died with him, we will also live with him; ¹² if we endure, we will also reign with him. If we disown him, he will also disown us; ¹³ if we are faithless, he remains faithful, for he cannot disown himself.

（提摩太後書；2章，11-13節）

¹¹ 有可信的話說：我們若與基督同死，也必與他同活；¹² 我們若能忍耐，也必和他一同作王；我們若不認他，他也必不認我們；¹³ 我們縱然失信，他仍是可信的，因為他不能背乎自己。

Vocabulary

trustworthy [ˈtrʌstˌwɝði] adj. 可靠的
endure [ɪnˈdʊr] v. 忍受
disown [dɪsˈon] v. 聲明與…斷絕關係
remain [rɪˈmen] v. 仍然是

saying [ˈseɪŋ] n. 說話；格言
reign [ren] v. 統治
faithless [ˈfeθləs] adj. 不忠實的

Here is a trustworthy saying: If we died with him, we will also live with him; if we endure, we will also reign with him. If we disown him, he will also disown us; if we are faithless, he remains faithful, for he cannot disown himself.

Day 93
神的應許信實
God's Promise Is Faithful

(Hebrews; Chapter 10: Verse 22-23)

²² let us draw near to God with a sincere heart and with the full assurance that faith brings, having our hearts sprinkled to cleanse us from a guilty conscience and having our bodies washed with pure water. ²³ Let us hold unswervingly to the hope we profess, for he who promised is faithful.

（希伯來書；10章，22-23節）

²² 並我們心中天良的虧欠已經灑去，身體用清水洗淨了，就當存著誠心和充足的信心來到神面前；²³ 也要堅守我們所承認的指望，不至搖動，因為那應許我們的是信實的。

Vocabulary

draw near 靠近	sincere [sɪnˈsɪr] adj. 真誠的
heart [hɑrt] n. 心	assurance [əˈʃʊrəns] n. 保證；信心
faith [feθ] n. 信心	cleanse [klɛnz] v. 清潔
guilty [ˈgɪlti] adj. 有罪的	conscience [ˈkɑnʃəns] n. 良心
pure [pjʊr] adj. 純淨的	hope [hop] n. 希望

let us draw near to God with a sincere heart and with the full assurance that faith brings, having our hearts sprinkled to cleanse us from a guilty conscience and having our bodies washed with pure water. Let us hold unswervingly to the hope we profess, for he who promised is faithful.

Day 94

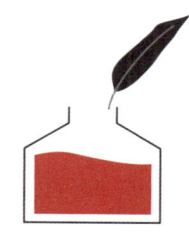

與信實神有分
Faithful God Calls You into Fellowship

(1 Corinthians; Chapter 1: Verse 8-9)

⁸ He will also keep you firm to the end, so that you will be blameless on the day of our Lord Jesus Christ. ⁹ God is faithful, who has called you into fellowship with his Son, Jesus Christ our Lord.

（哥林多前書；1章，8-9節）

⁸ 祂也必堅固你們到底，叫你們在我們主耶穌基督的日子無可責備。⁹ 神是信實的，你們原是被祂所召，好與祂兒子——我們的主耶穌基督一同得分。

Vocabulary

keep [kip] v. 保持
end [ɛnd] n. 結束
fellowship [ˈfɛləʊˌʃɪp] n. 夥伴關係；交情
firm [fɝm] adj. 堅定的
blameless [ˈblemləs] adj. 無可指責的
call [kɔl] v. 召喚

He will also keep you firm to the end, so that you will be blameless on the day of our Lord Jesus Christ. God is faithful, who has called you into fellowship with his Son, Jesus Christ our Lord.

Day 95
信實直到萬代
Faithfulness through All Generations

(Psalm 100: Verse 4-5)

⁴ Enter his gates with thanksgiving and his courts with praise; give thanks to him and praise his name. ⁵ For the Lord is good and his love endures forever; his faithfulness continues through all generations.

（詩篇；100 篇，4-5 節）

⁴ 當稱謝進入他的門；當讚美進入他的院。當感謝他，稱頌他的名！⁵ 因為耶和華本為善。祂的慈愛存到永遠；祂的信實直到萬代。

Vocabulary

enter [ˈɛntɚ] v. 進入
thanksgiving [θæŋksˈgɪvɪŋ] n. 感恩
praise [prez] v. 讚美
endure [ɪnˈdʊr] v. 持續
continue [kənˈtɪnju] v. 持續

gate [get] n. 大門
court [kɔrt] n. 庭院
name [nem] n. 名字
faithfulness [ˈfeθfəlnəs] n. 忠誠

Enter his gates with thanksgiving and his courts with praise; give thanks to him and praise his name. For the Lord is good and his love endures forever; his faithfulness continues through all generations.

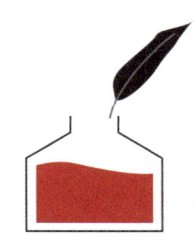

Day 96
信實堅立於天
Faithfulness Is Established in Heaven

(Psalm 89: Verse 1-2)

¹ I will sing of the Lord's great love forever; with my mouth I will make your faithfulness known through all generations. ² I will declare that your love stands firm forever, that you have established your faithfulness in heaven itself.

（詩篇；89篇，1-2節）

¹ 我要歌唱耶和華的慈愛，直到永遠；我要用口將祢的信實傳與萬代。² 因我曾說：祢的慈悲必建立到永遠；祢的信實必堅立在天上。

Vocabulary

- sing [sɪŋ] v. 唱
- forever [fəˈɛvɚ] adv. 永遠
- stand [stænd] v. 站立
- establish [ɪˈstæblɪʃ] v. 建立
- great [gret] adj. 偉大的
- declare [dɪˈklɛr] v. 宣布
- firm [fɝm] adj. 堅固的
- heaven [ˈhɛvn] n. 天國

I will sing of the Lord's great love forever; with my mouth I will make your faithfulness known through all generations. I will declare that your love stands firm forever, that you have established your faithfulness in heaven itself.

Day 97
信實為神所悅
God Delights Trustworthy People

(Proverbs; Chapter 12: Verse 22-24)

²² The Lord detests lying lips, but he delights in people who are trustworthy. ²³ The prudent keep their knowledge to themselves, but a fool's heart blurts out folly. ²⁴ Diligent hands will rule, but laziness ends in forced labor.

（箴言；12章，22-24節）

²² 說謊言的嘴為耶和華所憎惡；行事誠實的，為祂所喜悅。²³ 通達人隱藏知識；愚昧人的心彰顯愚昧。²⁴ 殷勤人的手必掌權；懶惰的人必服苦。

Vocabulary

detest [dɪˈtɛst] v. 厭惡	lying [ˈlaɪɪŋ] adj. 說謊的
lips [lɪps] n. 嘴唇	delight [dɪˈlaɪt] v. 愉悅
trustworthy [ˈtrʌstwɝðɪ] adj. 可靠的	prudent [ˈprudnt] adj. 精明的
knowledge [ˈnɑlɪdʒ] n. 知識	fool [ful] n. 愚人
diligent [ˈdɪlədʒənt] adj. 勤勞的	laziness [ˈlezɪnəs] n. 懶惰

The Lord detests lying lips, but he delights in people who are trustworthy. The prudent keep their knowledge to themselves, but a fool's heart blurts out folly. Diligent hands will rule, but laziness ends in forced labor.

Day 98

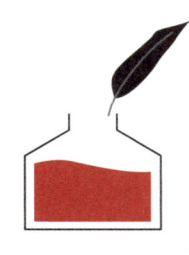

信實脫離惡者
Faithfulness Protects You from the Evil One

(2 Thessalonians; Chapter 3: Verse 3-4)

³ But the Lord is faithful, and he will strengthen you and protect you from the evil one. ⁴ We have confidence in the Lord that you are doing and will continue to do the things we command.

（帖撒羅尼迦後書；3章，3-4節）

³ 但主是信實的，要堅固你們，保護你們脫離那惡者（或作：脫離兇惡）。⁴ 我們靠主深信，你們現在是遵行我們所吩咐的，後來也必要遵行。

Vocabulary

faithful [ˈfeθfəl] adj. 忠實的
protect [prəˈtɛkt] v. 保護
confidence [ˈkɑnfədəns] n. 信心
thing [θɪŋ] n. 事情
strengthen [ˈstrɛŋθən] v. 加強
evil [ˈivəl] adj. 邪惡的
continue [kənˈtɪn.ju] v. 繼續
command [kəˈmænd] v. 命令

But the Lord is faithful, and he will strengthen you and protect you from the evil one. We have confidence in the Lord that you are doing and will continue to do the things we command.

Day 99
信實無可指摘
Become Blameless and Pure

(Philippians; Chapter 2: Verse 14-16)

¹⁴ Do everything without grumbling or arguing, ¹⁵ so that you may become blameless and pure, "children of God without fault in a warped and crooked generation." Then you will shine among them like stars in the sky ¹⁶ as you hold firmly to the word of life. And then I will be able to boast on the day of Christ that I did not run or labor in vain.

（腓立比書；2章，14-16節）

¹⁴ 凡所行的，都不要發怨言，起爭論，¹⁵ 使你們無可指摘，誠實無偽，在這彎曲悖謬的世代作神無瑕疵的兒女。你們顯在這世代中，好像明光照耀，¹⁶ 將生命的道表明出來，叫我在基督的日子好誇我沒有空跑，也沒有徒勞。

Vocabulary

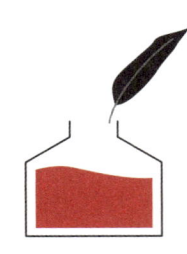

grumble [ˈgrʌmbəl] v. 抱怨	argue [ˈɑrgju] v. 爭論
blameless [ˈblemləs] adj. 無可指責的	pure [pjʊr] adj. 純潔的
children [ˈtʃɪldrən] n. 孩子們	generation [ˌdʒɛnəˈreɪʃən] n. 世代
shine [ʃaɪn] v. 閃耀	star [stɑr] n. 星星
firmly [ˈfɝmli] adv. 堅定地	boast [bost] v. 自誇
labor [ˈlebɚ] v. 勞動	in vain 徒勞地

Do everything without grumbling or arguing, so that you may become blameless and pure, "children of God without fault in a warped and crooked generation." Then you will shine among them like stars in the sky as you hold firmly to the word of life. And then I will be able to boast on the day of Christ that I did not run or labor in vain.

Day 100
信實認真傳道
God's Message Is "Yes"

(2 Corinthians; Chapter 1: Verse 18-19)

¹⁸ But as surely as God is faithful, our message to you is not "Yes" and "No." ¹⁹ For the Son of God, Jesus Christ, who was preached among you by us—by me and Silas and Timothy—was not "Yes" and "No," but in him it has always been "Yes."

（哥林多後書；1章，18-19節）

¹⁸ 我指著信實的神說，我們向你們所傳的道，並沒有是而又非的。¹⁹ 因為我和西拉並提摩太，在你們中間所傳神的兒子耶穌基督，總沒有是而又非的，在祂只有一是。

Vocabulary

surely [ˈʃʊrli] adv. 確實地
preach [priːtʃ] v. 講道
always [ˈɔlwez] adv. 總是
message [ˈmɛsɪdʒ] n. 訊息
among [əˈmʌŋ] prep. 在…（群體）中

But as surely as God is faithful, our message to you is not "Yes" and "No." For the Son of God, Jesus Christ, who was preached among you by us—by me and Silas and Timothy—was not "Yes" and "No," but in him it has always been "Yes."

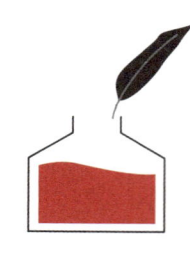

Day 101
愛心說誠實話
Speaking the Truth in Love

(Ephesians; Chapter 4: Verse 15-16)

¹⁵ Instead, speaking the truth in love, we will grow to become in every respect the mature body of him who is the head, that is, Christ. ¹⁶ From him the whole body, joined and held together by every supporting ligament, grows and builds itself up in love, as each part does its work.

（以弗所書；4 章，15-16 節）

¹⁵ 惟用愛心說誠實話，凡事長進，連於元首基督，¹⁶ 全身都靠祂聯絡得合式，百節各按各職，照著各體的功用彼此相助，便叫身體漸漸增長，在愛中建立自己。

Vocabulary

speak [ˈspiːk] v. 說（話）	truth [truθ] n. 實話
love [lʌv] n. 愛	grow [gro] v. 成長
become [bɪˈkʌm] v. 成為	mature [məˈtʃʊr] adj. 成熟的
body [ˈbɑdɪ] n. 身體	joined [dʒɔɪnd] adj. 連接的
ligament [ˈlɪgəmənt] n. 韌帶	build [bɪld] v. 建造

Instead, speaking the truth in love, we will grow to become in every respect the mature body of him who is the head, that is, Christ. From him the whole body, joined and held together by every supporting ligament, grows and builds itself up in love, as each part does its work.

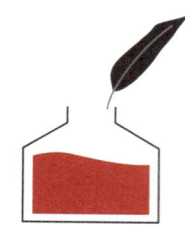

Day 102

與鄰信實相交
Speak the Truth to Each Other

(Zechariah; Chapter 8: Verse 16-17)

¹⁶ These are the things you are to do: Speak the truth to each other, and render true and sound judgment in your courts; ¹⁷ do not plot evil against each other, and do not love to swear falsely. I hate all this," declares the Lord.

（撒迦利亞書；8章，16-17節）

¹⁶ 你們所當行的是這樣：各人與鄰舍說話誠實，在城門口按至理判斷，使人和睦。¹⁷ 誰都不可心裡謀害鄰舍，也不可喜愛起假誓，因為這些事都為我所恨惡。這是耶和華說的。

Vocabulary

each other 互相，彼此	**render** [ˈrɛndɚ] **v.** 表達；使處於某種狀態
judgment [ˈdʒʌdʒmənt] **n.** 判斷	**plot** [plɑt] **v.** 策劃
swear [swɛr] **v.** 發（誓）	**falsely** [ˈfɔlslɪ] **adv.** 虛假地
declare [dɪˈklɛr] **v.** 宣告	

These are the things you are to do: Speak the truth to each other, and render true and sound judgment in your courts; do not plot evil against each other, and do not love to swear falsely. I hate all this," declares the Lord.

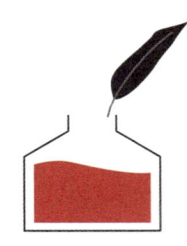

Day 103
說話是非分明
Say Simply 'Yes' or 'No'

(Matthew; Chapter 5: Verse 34-37)

³⁴ But I tell you, do not swear an oath at all: either by heaven, for it is God's throne; ³⁵ or by the earth, for it is his footstool; or by Jerusalem, for it is the city of the Great King. ³⁶ And do not swear by your head, for you cannot make even one hair white or black. ³⁷ All you need to say is simply 'Yes' or 'No'; anything beyond this comes from the evil one.

（馬太福音；5 章，34-37 節）

³⁴ 只是我告訴你們，什麼誓都不可起。不可指著天起誓，因為天是神的座位；³⁵ 不可指著地起誓，因為地是祂的腳凳；也不可指著耶路撒冷起誓，因為耶路撒冷是大君的京城；³⁶ 又不可指著你的頭起誓，因為你不能使一根頭髮變黑變白了。³⁷ 你們的話，是，就說是；不是，就說不是；若再多說，就是出於那惡者（或作：就是從惡裡出來的）。

Vocabulary

swear [swɛr] v. 發（誓）
heaven [ˈhɛvn] n. 天空
earth [ɝθ] n. 地面
head [hɛd] n. 頭

oath [oθ] n. 誓言
throne [θron] n. 王座
footstool [ˈfʊtˌstul] n. 腳凳
city [ˈsɪtɪ] n. 城市

But I tell you, do not swear an oath at all: either by heaven, for it is God's throne; or by the earth, for it is his footstool; or by Jerusalem, for it is the city of the Great King. And do not swear by your head, for you cannot make even one hair white or black. All you need to say is simply 'Yes' or 'No'; anything beyond this comes from the evil one.

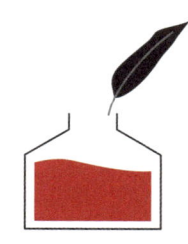

Day 104
不可假冒為善 Don't Be Hypocrites

(Matthew; Chapter 23: Verse 23)

23 "Woe to you, teachers of the law and Pharisees, you hypocrites! You give a tenth of your spices—mint, dill and cumin. But you have neglected the more important matters of the law—justice, mercy and faithfulness. You should have practiced the latter, without neglecting the former.

（馬太福音；23章，23節）

23 你們這假冒為善的文士和法利賽人有禍了！因為你們將薄荷、茴香、芹菜，獻上十分之一，那律法上更重的事，就是公義、憐憫、信實，反倒不行了。這更重的是你們當行的；那也是不可不行的。

Vocabulary

woe [wo] n. 悲哀	teacher [ˈtitʃɚ] n. 老師
law [lɔ] n. 律法	Pharisees [ˈfærəˌsiz] n. 法利賽人
hypocrite [ˈhɪpəˌkrɪt] n. 偽君子	spice [ˈspaɪs] n. 香料
neglect [nɪˈɡlɛkt] v. 忽略	important [ɪmˈpɔrtənt] adj. 重要的
justice [ˈdʒʌstɪs] n. 公義	mercy [ˈmɝsɪ] n. 憐憫

"Woe to you, teachers of the law and Pharisees, you hypocrites! You give a tenth of your spices—mint, dill and cumin. But you have neglected the more important matters of the law—justice, mercy and faithfulness. You should have practiced the latter, without neglecting the former.

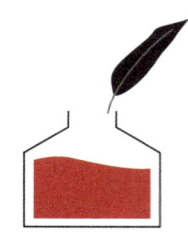

Day 105
向信實神認罪 Confess Our Sins

(1 John; Chapter 1: Verse 8-9)

⁸ If we claim to be without sin, we deceive ourselves and the truth is not in us. ⁹ If we confess our sins, he is faithful and just and will forgive us our sins and purify us from all unrighteousness.

（約翰一書；1章，8-9節）

⁸ 我們若說自己無罪，便是自欺，真理不在我們心裡了。⁹ 我們若認自己的罪，神是信實的，是公義的，必要赦免我們的罪，洗淨我們一切的不義。

Vocabulary

claim [klem] v. 聲稱	sin [sɪn] n. 罪
deceive [dɪˈsiv] v. 欺騙	truth [truθ] n. 真理
confess [kənˈfɛs] v. 承認	just [dʒʌst] adj. 公正的
forgive [fɚˈgɪv] v. 寬恕，原諒	purify [ˈpjʊrəfaɪ] v. 淨化

If we claim to be without sin, we deceive ourselves and the truth is not in us. If we confess our sins, he is faithful and just and will forgive us our sins and purify us from all unrighteousness.

自我反思

我們一起完成了信實篇 15 天的閱讀與抄寫，現在就透過以下問題來看看各位所獲得的成果。

- 在信實篇中，最令您印象深刻的金句是哪一句？

....
....
....
....

- 這 15 天的單元中，您最喜歡哪一天的內容？為什麼？

....
....
....
....
....

Chapter 8
溫柔

(James; Chapter 1: Verse 21)

21 Therefore, get rid of all moral filth and the evil that is so prevalent and humbly accept the word planted in you, which can save you.

（雅各書；1章，21節）

21 所以你們要脫去一切的污穢和盈餘的邪惡，存溫柔的心領受那所栽種的道，就是能救你們靈魂的道。

Day 106
溫柔的人承受地土
The Meek Inherit the Earth

(Matthew; Chapter 5: Verse 4-6)

⁴ Blessed are those who mourn, for they will be comforted. ⁵ Blessed are the meek, for they will inherit the earth. ⁶ Blessed are those who hunger and thirst for righteousness, for they will be filled.

（馬太福音；5 章，4-6 節）

⁴ 哀慟的人有福了！因為他們必得安慰。⁵ 溫柔的人有福了！因為他們必承受地土。⁶ 飢渴慕義的人有福了！因為他們必得飽足。

Vocabulary

blessed [ˈblɛst] **adj.** 有福的
comfort [ˈkʌmfɚt] **v.** 安慰
inherit [ɪnˈhɛrɪt] **v.** 繼承
hunger [ˈhʌŋgɚ] **v.** 飢餓
righteousness [ˈraɪtʃəsnəs] **n.** 公義

mourn [mɔrn] **v.** 哀悼
meek [mik] **adj.** 溫順的
earth [ɝθ] **n.** 土地
thirst [θɝst] **v.** 口渴

Blessed are those who mourn, for they will be comforted. Blessed are the meek, for they will inherit the earth. Blessed are those who hunger and thirst for righteousness, for they will be filled.

Day 107
效主溫柔得享安息
Learn from God's Gentleness

(Matthew; Chapter 11: Verse 28-30)

²⁸ "Come to me, all you who are weary and burdened, and I will give you rest. ²⁹ Take my yoke upon you and learn from me, for I am gentle and humble in heart, and you will find rest for your souls. ³⁰ For my yoke is easy and my burden is light."

（馬太福音；11章，28-30節）

²⁸ 凡勞苦擔重擔的人可以到我這裡來，我就使你們得安息。²⁹ 我心裡柔和謙卑，你們當負我的軛，學我的樣式；這樣，你們心裡就必得享安息。³⁰ 因為我的軛是容易的，我的擔子是輕省的。

Vocabulary

weary [ˈwɪri] adj. 疲倦的
rest [rɛst] n. 休息
learn [lɝn] v. 學習
humble [ˈhʌmbəl] adj. 謙卑的
easy [ˈizɪ] adj. 容易的

burden [ˈbɝdən] v. 負擔
yoke [jok] n. 牛軛；束縛
gentle [ˈdʒɛntl] adj. 溫柔的
heart [hart] n. 心
light [laɪt] adj. 輕的

"Come to me, all you who are weary and burdened, and I will give you rest. Take my yoke upon you and learn from me, for I am gentle and humble in heart, and you will find rest for your souls. For my yoke is easy and my burden is light."

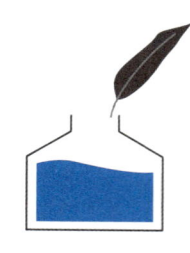

Day 108
保羅傳道溫柔勸戒
Paul's Preach Is Gentle

(2 Corinthians; Chapter 10: Verse 1-2)

¹ By the humility and gentleness of Christ, I appeal to you—I, Paul, who am "timid" when face to face with you, but "bold" toward you when away! ² I beg you that when I come I may not have to be as bold as I expect to be toward some people who think that we live by the standards of this world.

（哥林多後書；10章，1-2節）

¹ 我保羅，就是與你們見面的時候是謙卑的，不在你們那裡的時候向你們是勇敢的，如今親自藉著基督的溫柔、和平勸你們。² 有人以為我是憑著血氣行事，我也以為必須用勇敢待這等人；求你們不要叫我在你們那裡的時候，有這樣的勇敢。

Vocabulary

humility [hjuˈmɪlətɪ] **n.** 謙遜	gentleness [ˈdʒɛntlnəs] **n.** 溫柔
timid [ˈtɪmɪd] **adj.** 怯懦的	bold [bold] **adj.** 大膽的
appeal to 呼籲	beg [bɛg] **v.** 懇求
expect [ɪkˈspɛkt] **v.** 預期	standard [ˈstændɚd] **n.** 標準

By the humility and gentleness of Christ, I appeal to you—I, Paul, who am "timid" when face to face with you, but "bold" toward you when away! I beg you that when I come I may not have to be as bold as I expect to be toward some people who think that we live by the standards of this world.

Day 109

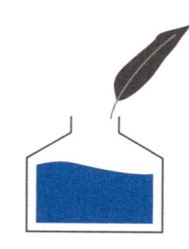

內心溫柔極其寶貴
Gentle Inner Is Great in God's Sight

(1 Peter; Chapter 3: Verse 3-4)

³ Your beauty should not come from outward adornment, such as elaborate hairstyles and the wearing of gold jewelry or fine clothes. ⁴ Rather, it should be that of your inner self, the unfading beauty of a gentle and quiet spirit, which is of great worth in God's sight.

（彼得前書；3章，3-4節）

³你們不要以外面的辮頭髮，戴金飾，穿美衣為妝飾，⁴只要以裡面存著長久溫柔，安靜的心為妝飾；這在神面前是極寶貴的。

Vocabulary

beauty [ˈbjutɪ] **n.** 美麗
adornment [əˈdɔrnmənt] **n.** 裝飾
hairstyle [ˈhɛrˌstaɪl] **n.** 髮型
inner [ˈɪnɚ] **adj.** 內在的
quiet [ˈkwaɪət] **adj.** 安靜的

outward [ˈaʊtwɚd] **adj.** 外在的
elaborate [ɪˈlæbəˌret] **adj.** 精緻的
jewelry [ˈdʒuəlrɪ] **n.** 珠寶
unfading [ʌnˈfedɪŋ] **adj.** 不褪色的，不凋零的

Your beauty should not come from outward adornment, such as elaborate hairstyles and the wearing of gold jewelry or fine clothes. Rather, it should be that of your inner self, the unfading beauty of a gentle and quiet spirit, which is of great worth in God's sight.

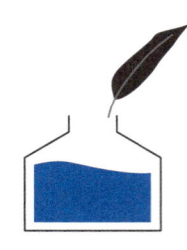

Day 110

性情溫良是有聰明
Even-tempered One Has Understanding

(Proverbs; Chapter 17: Verse 27-28)

27 The one who has knowledge uses words with restraint, and whoever has understanding is even-tempered. **28** Even fools are thought wise if they keep silent, and discerning if they hold their tongues.

（箴言；17 章，27-28 節）

27 寡少言語的，有知識；性情溫良的，有聰明。**28** 愚昧人若靜默不言也可算為智慧；閉口不說也可算為聰明。

Vocabulary

knowledge [ˈnɑlɪdʒ] **n.** 知識
understanding [ˌʌndɚˈstændɪŋ] **n.** 理解
wise [waɪz] **adj.** 智慧的
silent [ˈsaɪlənt] **adj.** 沉默的
restraint [rɪˈstrent] **n.** 節制
even-tempered [ˌivənˈtɛmpɚd] **adj.** 性情溫和的
discern [dɪˈsɜn] **v.** 辨別出

The one who has knowledge uses words with restraint, and whoever has understanding is even-tempered. Even fools are thought wise if they keep silent, and discerning if they hold their tongues.

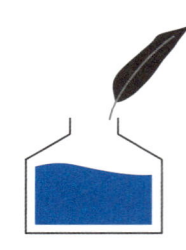

Day 111

快聽慢說慢慢動怒
Quick to Listen, Slow to Speak and Slow to Become Angry

(James; Chapter 1: Verse 19-20)

[19] My dear brothers and sisters, take note of this: Everyone should be quick to listen, slow to speak and slow to become angry, [20] because human anger does not produce the righteousness that God desires.

（雅各書；1章，19-20節）

[19] 我親愛的弟兄們，這是你們所知道的，但你們各人要快快的聽，慢慢的說，慢慢的動怒，[20] 因為人的怒氣並不成就神的義。

Vocabulary

quick [kwɪk] adj. 迅速的
slow [slo] adj. 慢的
angry [ˈæŋgrɪ] adj. 生氣的
produce [prəˋdjus] v. 產生

listen [ˈlɪsən] v. 聆聽
speak [spiːk] v. 說話
human [ˈhjuːmən] adj. 人的
righteousness [ˈraɪtʃəsnəs] n. 公義

My dear brothers and sisters, take note of this: Everyone should be quick to listen, slow to speak and slow to become angry, because human anger does not produce the righteousness that God desires.

Day 112

尊主為聖溫柔回答
Revere the LORD and Answer Gentlely

(1 Peter; Chapter 3: Verse 14-15)

¹⁴ But even if you should suffer for what is right, you are blessed. "Do not fear their threats; do not be frightened." ¹⁵ But in your hearts revere Christ as Lord. Always be prepared to give an answer to everyone who asks you to give the reason for the hope that you have. But do this with gentleness and respect,

（彼得前書；3章，14-15節）

¹⁴ 你們就是為義受苦，也是有福的。不要怕人的威嚇（或作：所怕的），也不要驚慌；¹⁵ 只要心裡尊主基督為聖。有人問你們心中盼望的緣由，就要常作準備，以溫柔、敬畏的心回答各人；

Vocabulary

suffer [ˈsʌfɚ] **v.** 受苦	right [raɪt] **adj.** 正義的
fear [fɪr] **v.** 害怕	threat [θrɛt] **n.** 威脅
frighten [ˈfraɪtn] **v.** 使害怕	revere [rɪˈvɪr] **v.** 崇敬
answer [ˈænsɚ] **n.** 回答	hope [hop] **n.** 希望

But even if you should suffer for what is right, you are blessed. "Do not fear their threats; do not be frightened." But in your hearts revere Christ as Lord. Always be prepared to give an answer to everyone who asks you to give the reason for the hope that you have. But do this with gentleness and respect,

Day 113

溫良的舌是生命樹
Soothing Tongue Is a Tree of Life

(Proverbs; Chapter 15: Verse 4-6)

⁴ The soothing tongue is a tree of life, but a perverse tongue crushes the spirit. ⁵ A fool spurns a parent's discipline, but whoever heeds correction shows prudence. ⁶ The house of the righteous contains great treasure, but the income of the wicked brings ruin.

（箴言；15章，4-6節）

⁴ 溫良的舌是生命樹；乖謬的嘴使人心碎。⁵ 愚妄人藐視父親的管教；領受責備的，得著見識。⁶ 義人家中多有財寶；惡人得利反受擾害。

Vocabulary

soothing [ˈsuðɪŋ] adj. 安慰的
perverse [pɚˈvɝs] adj. 反常的
spurn [spɝn] v. 輕蔑地拒絕
righteous [ˈraɪtʃəs] adj. 正義的
wicked [ˈwɪkɪd] adj. 邪惡的
tongue [tʌŋ] n. 舌頭
crush [ˈkrʌʃ] v. 壓碎
discipline [ˈdɪsəplɪn] n. 紀律
treasure [ˈtrɛʒɚ] n. 寶藏

The soothing tongue is a tree of life, but a perverse tongue crushes the spirit. A fool spurns a parent's discipline, but whoever heeds correction shows prudence. The house of the righteous contains great treasure, but the income of the wicked brings ruin.

Day 114
溫柔回答使怒消退
Gentle Answer Turns Away Wrath

(Proverbs; Chapter 15: Verse 1-3)

¹ A gentle answer turns away wrath, but a harsh word stirs up anger. ² The tongue of the wise adorns knowledge, but the mouth of the fool gushes folly. ³ The eyes of the Lord are everywhere, keeping watch on the wicked and the good.

（箴言；15章，1-3節）

¹ 回答柔和，使怒消退；言語暴戾，觸動怒氣。² 智慧人的舌善發知識；愚昧人的口吐出愚昧。³ 耶和華的眼目無處不在；惡人善人，祂都鑒察。

Vocabulary

gentle [ˈdʒɛntl] adj. 溫柔的	wrath [ræθ] n. 憤怒
harsh [hɑrʃ] adj. 嚴厲的	stir up 激起，挑起，煽動
anger [ˈæŋɡɚ] n. 憤怒	adorn [əˈdɔrn] v. 裝飾
gush [ɡʌʃ] v. 湧出，冒出	folly [ˈfɑlɪ] n. 愚蠢
wicked [ˈwɪkɪd] adj. 邪惡的	

A gentle answer turns away wrath, but a harsh word stirs up anger. The tongue of the wise adorns knowledge, but the mouth of the fool gushes folly. The eyes of the Lord are everywhere, keeping watch on the wicked and the good.

Day 115
智慧溫柔顯出善行
Show Good Deeds in Wisdom and Humility

(James; Chapter 3: Verse 13-14)

¹³ Who is wise and understanding among you? Let them show it by their good life, by deeds done in the humility that comes from wisdom. ¹⁴ But if you harbor bitter envy and selfish ambition in your hearts, do not boast about it or deny the truth.

（雅各書；3章，13-14節）

¹³ 你們中間誰是有智慧有見識的呢？他就當在智慧的溫柔上顯出他的善行來。¹⁴ 你們心裡若懷著苦毒的嫉妒和分爭，就不可自誇，也不可說謊話抵擋真道。

Vocabulary

- wise [waɪz] **adj.** 智慧的
- deeds [diːdz] **n.** 行為
- harbor [ˈhɑrbɚ] **v.** 懷有
- envy [ˈɛnvɪ] **n.** 嫉妒
- ambition [æmˈbɪʃən] **n.** 野心
- truth [truθ] **n.** 真理
- understanding [ˌʌndɚˈstændɪŋ] **adj.** 通情達理的
- humility [hjuˈmɪlətɪ] **n.** 謙卑
- bitter [ˈbɪtɚ] **adj.** 苦的
- selfish [ˈsɛlfɪʃ] **adj.** 自私的
- boast [bost] **v.** 自誇

Who is wise and understanding among you? Let them show it by their good life, by deeds done in the humility that comes from wisdom. But if you harbor bitter envy and selfish ambition in your hearts, do not boast about it or deny the truth.

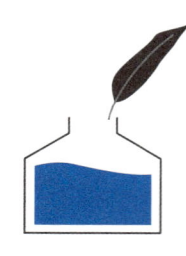

Day 116
溫柔忍耐愛心寬容
Bear Others in Gentle Love

(Ephesians; Chapter 4: Verse 2-4)

² Be completely humble and gentle; be patient, bearing with one another in love. ³ Make every effort to keep the unity of the Spirit through the bond of peace. ⁴ There is one body and one Spirit, just as you were called to one hope when you were called;

（以弗所書；4章，2-4節）

² 凡事謙虛、溫柔、忍耐，用愛心互相寬容，³ 用和平彼此聯絡，竭力保守聖靈所賜合而為一的心。⁴ 身體只有一個，聖靈只有一個，正如你們蒙召同有一個指望；

Vocabulary

completely [kəmˈplitlɪ] adv. 完全地	humble [ˈhʌmbəl] adj. 謙卑的
gentle [ˈdʒɛntl] adj. 溫柔的	patient [ˈpeʃənt] adj. 耐心的
bear [ˈbɛr] v. 忍受	love [lʌv] n. 愛
effort [ˈɛfɚt] n. 努力	unity [ˈjuːnətɪ] n. 團結
bond [band] n. 聯繫	peace [pis] n. 和平

Be completely humble and gentle; be patient, bearing with one another in love. Make every effort to keep the unity of the Spirit through the bond of peace. There is one body and one Spirit, just as you were called to one hope when you were called;

Day 117

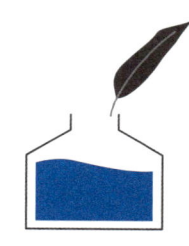

溫和待人善於教導
Kind to Everyone, Able to Teach

(2 Timothy; Chapter 2: Verse 24-25)

24 And the Lord's servant must not be quarrelsome but must be kind to everyone, able to teach, not resentful. **25** Opponents must be gently instructed, in the hope that God will grant them repentance leading them to a knowledge of the truth,

（提摩太後書；2章，24-25節）

24 然而主的僕人不可爭競，只要溫溫和和的待眾人，善於教導，存心忍耐，**25** 用溫柔勸戒那抵擋的人；或者神給他們悔改的心，可以明白真道，

Vocabulary

servant [ˈsɝvənt] **n.** 僕人
kind [kaɪnd] **adj.** 仁慈的
resentful [rɪˈzɛntfəl] **adj.** 憤恨的
repentance [rɪˈpɛntəns] **n.** 懺悔

quarrelsome [ˈkwɔrəlˌsəm] **adj.** 好爭吵的
teach [titʃ] **v.** 教導
opponent [əˈponənt] **n.** 對手

And the Lord's servant must not be quarrelsome but must be kind to everyone, able to teach, not resentful. Opponents must be gently instructed, in the hope that God will grant them repentance leading them to a knowledge of the truth,

Day 118

溫柔持家兒女順服
Not Violent but Gentle in Managing the Family

(1 Timothy; Chapter 3: Verse 3-5)

³ not given to drunkenness, not violent but gentle, not quarrelsome, not a lover of money. ⁴ He must manage his own family well and see that his children obey him, and he must do so in a manner worthy of full respect. ⁵ (If anyone does not know how to manage his own family, how can he take care of God's church?)

（提摩太前書；3章，3-5節）

³ 不因酒滋事，不打人，只要溫和，不爭競，不貪財；⁴ 好好管理自己的家，使兒女凡事端莊順服（或作：端端莊莊地使兒女順服）。⁵ 人若不知道管理自己的家，焉能照管神的教會呢？

Vocabulary

drunkenness [ˈdrʌŋkənnɪs] n. 酗酒
gentle [ˈdʒɛntl] adj. 溫柔的
lover [ˈlʌvɚ] n. 愛好者
family [ˈfæməlɪ] n. 家庭
respect [rɪˈspɛkt] n. 尊重

violent [ˈvaɪələnt] adj. 暴力的
quarrelsome [ˈkwɔrəlˌsəm] adj. 好爭吵的
manage [ˈmænɪdʒ] v. 管理
obey [əˈbe] v. 服從

not given to drunkenness, not violent but gentle, not quarrelsome, not a lover of money. He must manage his own family well and see that his children obey him, and he must do so in a manner worthy of full respect. (If anyone does not know how to manage his own family, how can he take care of God's church?)

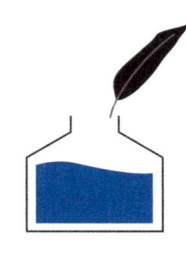

Day 119

存心溫柔照顧信徒
Care for Believers Like a Nursing Mother

(1 Thessalonians; Chapter 2: Verse 6-7)

⁶ We were not looking for praise from people, not from you or anyone else, even though as apostles of Christ we could have asserted our authority. ⁷ Instead, we were like young children among you. Just as a nursing mother cares for her children,

（帖撒羅尼迦前書；2章，6-7節）

⁶ 我們作基督的使徒，雖然可以叫人尊重，卻沒有向你們或向別人求榮耀；⁷ 只在你們中間存心溫柔，如同母親乳養自己的孩子。

Vocabulary

look for 尋找
apostle [əˈpɑstəl] n. 使徒
authority [əˈθɔrətɪ] n. 權威
children [ˈtʃɪldrən] n. 孩子們

praise [prez] n. 讚美
assert [əˈsɝt] v. 聲稱
young [jʌŋ] adj. 年輕的
care for 照顧，照料

We were not looking for praise from people, not from you or anyone else, even though as apostles of Christ we could have asserted our authority. Instead, we were like young children among you. Just as a nursing mother cares for her children,

Day 120
用溫柔心挽回信徒
Restore Believers Gently

(Galatians; Chapter 6: Verse 1-2)

¹ Brothers and sisters, if someone is caught in a sin, you who live by the Spirit should restore that person gently. But watch yourselves, or you also may be tempted. ² Carry each other's burdens, and in this way you will fulfill the law of Christ.

（加拉太書；6章，1-2節）

¹ 弟兄們，若有人偶然被過犯所勝，你們屬靈的人就當用溫柔的心把他挽回過來；又當自己小心，恐怕也被引誘。² 你們各人的重擔要互相擔當，如此，就完全了基督的律法。

Vocabulary

caught [kɔt] v. (catch 的過去分詞) 被抓住	sin [sɪn] n. 罪
restore [rɪˋstor] v. 恢復	gently [ˋdʒɛntlɪ] adv. 溫柔地
watch [watʃ] v. 注意	tempt [ˋtɛmpt] v. 誘惑
burden [ˋbɝːdən] n. 負擔	fulfill [fʊlˋfɪl] 履行，完成，服從

Brothers and sisters, if someone is caught in a sin, you who live by the Spirit should restore that person gently. But watch yourselves, or you also may be tempted. Carry each other's burdens, and in this way you will fulfill the law of Christ.

自我反思

我們一起完成了溫柔篇 15 天的閱讀與抄寫,現在就透過以下問題來看看各位所獲得的成果。

- 在溫柔篇中,最令您印象深刻的金句是哪一句?

　

　

　

　

- 這 15 天的單元中,您最喜歡哪一天的內容?為什麼?

Chapter 9
節制

(Proverbs; Chapter 23: Verse 2)

²and put a knife to your throat if you are given to gluttony.

（箴言；23章，2節）

²你若是貪食的，就當拿刀放在喉嚨上。

Day 121
保守你心勝過一切
Above All Else, Guard Your Heart

(Proverbs; Chapter 4: Verse 23-25)

²³ Above all else, guard your heart, for everything you do flows from it. ²⁴ Keep your mouth free of perversity; keep corrupt talk far from your lips. ²⁵ Let your eyes look straight ahead; fix your gaze directly before you.

（箴言；4章，23-25節）

²³ 你要保守你心，勝過保守一切（或譯：你要切切保守你心），因為一生的果效是由心發出。²⁴ 你要除掉邪僻的口，棄絕乖謬的嘴。²⁵ 你的眼目要向前正看；你的眼睛（原文是皮）當向前直觀。

Vocabulary

- **guard** [gɑrd] **v.** 保護，守護
- **flow** [flo] **v.** 流動
- **corrupt** [kəˋrʌpt] **adj.** 腐敗的
- **lips** [lɪps] **n.** 嘴唇
- **gaze** [gez] **n.** 目光
- **heart** [hɑrt] **n.** 心
- **perversity** [pəˋvɝsətɪ] **n.** 墮落，邪惡
- **talk** [tɔk] **n.** 說話
- **straight** [stret] **adj.** 直的

Above all else, guard your heart, for everything you do flows from it. Keep your mouth free of perversity; keep corrupt talk far from your lips. Let your eyes look straight ahead; fix your gaze directly before you.

Day 122

約束己心謹慎自守
Be Alert and Fully Sober with Minds

(1 Peter; Chapter 1: Verse 13-14)

¹³ Therefore, with minds that are alert and fully sober, set your hope on the grace to be brought to you when Jesus Christ is revealed at his coming. ¹⁴ As obedient children, do not conform to the evil desires you had when you lived in ignorance.

（彼得前書；1 章，13-14 節）

¹³ 所以要約束你們的心（原文作束上你們心中的腰），謹慎自守，專心盼望耶穌基督顯現的時候所帶來給你們的恩。¹⁴ 你們既作順命的兒女，就不要效法從前蒙昧無知的時候那放縱私慾的樣子。

Vocabulary

alert [əˋlɝt] **adj.** 警覺的

hope [hop] **n.** 希望

reveal [rɪˋvil] **v.** 展現；顯示

conform to 遵從

ignorance [ˋɪɡnərəns] **n.** 無知

sober [ˋsobɚ] **adj.** 清醒的

grace [ɡres] **n.** 恩典

obedient [əˋbidjənt] **adj.** 順從的

evil [ˋivəl] **adj.** 邪惡的

Therefore, with minds that are alert and fully sober, set your hope on the grace to be brought to you when Jesus Christ is revealed at his coming. As obedient children, do not conform to the evil desires you had when you lived in ignorance.

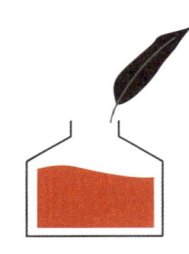

Day 123
制伏己心形同固牆
Lacking Self-control Is Like a City with Broken Walls

(Proverbs; Chapter 25: Verse 27-28)

²⁷ It is not good to eat too much honey, nor is it honorable to search out matters that are too deep. ²⁸ Like a city whose walls are broken through is a person who lacks self-control.

（箴言；25章，27-28節）

²⁷ 吃蜜過多是不好的；考究自己的榮耀也是可厭的。²⁸ 人不制伏自己的心，好像毀壞的城邑沒有牆垣。

Vocabulary

eat [it] **v.** 吃	honey [ˈhʌnɪ] **n.** 蜂蜜
honorable [ˈɑnərəbəl] **adj.** 值得尊敬的	search out 探索
deep [dip] **adj.** 深的	city [ˈsɪtɪ] **n.** 城市
lack [læk] **v.** 缺乏	self-control [ˌsɛlfkənˈtrol] **n.** 自制力

It is not good to eat too much honey, nor is it honorable to search out matters that are too deep. Like a city whose walls are broken through is a person who lacks self-control.

Day 124

攻克己身叫身服我
Discipline the Body and Bring It into Subjection

(1 Corinthians; Chapter 9: Verse 26-27)

²⁶ Therefore I do not run like someone running aimlessly; I do not fight like a boxer beating the air. ²⁷ No, I strike a blow to my body and make it my slave so that after I have preached to others, I myself will not be disqualified for the prize.

（哥林多前書；9 章，26-27 節）

²⁶ 所以，我奔跑不像無定向的；我鬥拳不像打空氣的。²⁷ 我是攻克己身，叫身服我，恐怕我傳福音給別人，自己反被棄絕了。

Vocabulary

therefore [ˈðɛrfor] adv. 因此	run [rʌn] v. 跑
aimlessly [ˈemlɪslɪ] adv. 無目的地	fight [faɪt] v. 搏鬥，打鬥
boxer [ˈbɑksɚ] n. 拳擊手	beat [ˈbitɪŋ] v. 打，擊
strike [straɪk] v. 擊，打	blow [blo] n. 一擊
slave [slev] n. 奴隸	disqualify [ˌdɪskwɑləˈfaɪ] v. 取消資格

Therefore I do not run like someone running aimlessly; I do not fight like a boxer beating the air. No, I strike a blow to my body and make it my slave so that after I have preached to others, I myself will not be disqualified for the prize.

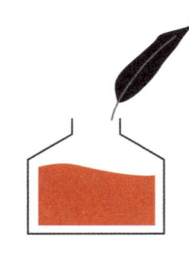

Day 125
世間享受都是虛空
Worldly Pleasures Are Meaningless

(Ecclesiastes; Chapter 2: Verse 10-11)

10 I denied myself nothing my eyes desired; I refused my heart no pleasure. My heart took delight in all my labor, and this was the reward for all my toil. **11** Yet when I surveyed all that my hands had done and what I had toiled to achieve, everything was meaningless, a chasing after the wind; nothing was gained under the sun.

（傳道書；2章，10-11節）

10 凡我眼所求的，我沒有留下不給他的；我心所樂的，我沒有禁止不享受的；因我的心為我一切所勞碌的快樂，這就是我從勞碌中所得的分。**11** 後來，我察看我手所經營的一切事和我勞碌所成的功。誰知都是虛空，都是捕風；在日光之下毫無益處。

Vocabulary

- deny [dɪˈnaɪ] v. 否認
- refuse [rɪˈfjuːz] v. 拒絕
- delight [dɪˈlaɪt] n. 喜悅
- reward [rɪˈwɔrd] n. 獎勵
- survey [səˈve] v. 審視，檢查
- meaningless [ˈminɪŋlɪs] adj. 毫無意義的
- gain [gen] v. 獲得
- desire [dɪˈzaɪr] v. 渴望
- pleasure [ˈplɛʒɚ] n. 快樂
- labor [ˈlebɚ] n. 勞動
- toil [tɔɪl] n. 辛勞
- achieve [əˈtʃiv] v. 達成
- chase [tʃes] v. 追逐

I denied myself nothing my eyes desired; I refused my heart no pleasure. My heart took delight in all my labor, and this was the reward for all my toil. Yet when I surveyed all that my hands had done and what I had toiled to achieve, everything was meaningless, a chasing after the wind; nothing was gained under the sun.

Day 126
有衣有食就當知足
Be Content with Having Food and Clothing

(1 Timothy; Chapter 6: Verse 6-8)

⁶ But godliness with contentment is great gain. ⁷ For we brought nothing into the world, and we can take nothing out of it. ⁸ But if we have food and clothing, we will be content with that.

（提摩太前書；6章，6-8節）

⁶ 然而，敬虔加上知足的心便是大利了；⁷ 因為我們沒有帶什麼到世上來，也不能帶什麼去。⁸ 只要有衣有食，就當知足。

Vocabulary

godliness [ˈgɑdlɪnəs] n. 虔誠
gain [gen] n. 收益，獲利
world [wɝld] n. 世界
clothing [ˈkloðɪŋ] n. 衣物
contentment [kənˈtɛntmənt] n. 滿足
brought [brɔt] v. （bring 的過去式）帶來
food [fud] n. 食物
content [kənˈtɛnt] adj. 滿足的

But godliness with contentment is great gain. For we brought nothing into the world, and we can take nothing out of it. But if we have food and clothing, we will be content with that.

Day 127

不看自己過於當看
Don't Think of Yourself More Highly Than You Ought

(Romans; Chapter 12: Verse 3)

³ For by the grace given me I say to every one of you: Do not think of yourself more highly than you ought, but rather think of yourself with sober judgment, in accordance with the faith God has distributed to each of you.

（羅馬書；12 章，3 節）

³ 我憑著所賜我的恩對你們各人說：不要看自己過於所當看的，要照著神所分給各人信心的大小，看得合乎中道。

Vocabulary

- grace [gres] **n.** 恩典
- highly [ˈhaɪlɪ] **adv.** 高度地
- sober [ˈsobɚ] **adj.** 清醒的
- in accordance with 依照
- think of 認為，覺得
- ought [ɔt] **aux.** 應該
- judgment [ˈdʒʌdʒmənt] **n.** 判斷
- distribute [dɪˈstrɪbjʊt] **v.** 分配

For by the grace given me I say to every one of you: Do not think of yourself more highly than you ought, but rather think of yourself with sober judgment, in accordance with the faith God has distributed to each of you.

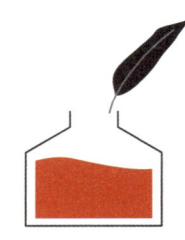

Day 128
不易發怒勝過勇士
Better a Patient Person Than a Warrior

(Proverbs; Chapter 16: Verse 32-33)

³² Better a patient person than a warrior, one with self-control than one who takes a city. ³³ The lot is cast into the lap, but its every decision is from the Lord.

（箴言；16 章，32-33 節）

³² 不輕易發怒的，勝過勇士；治服己心的，強如取城。³³ 籤放在懷裡，定事由耶和華。

Vocabulary

- **patient** [ˈpeʃənt] **adj.** 耐心的
- **self-control** [ˌsɛlfkənˈtrol] **n.** 自制力
- **lot** [lɑt] **n.** 命運，籤
- **lap** [læp] **n.** 膝部
- **warrior** [ˈwɔriɚ] **n.** 戰士
- **take** [tek] **v.** 佔有，取得
- **cast** [kæst] **v.** 拋，擲
- **decision** [dɪˈsɪʒən] **n.** 決定

Better a patient person than a warrior, one with self-control than one who takes a city. The lot is cast into the lap, but its every decision is from the Lord.

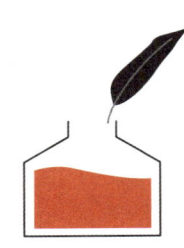

Day 129
節制貪念沒有愁苦
Love of Money Is a Root of Evil

(1 Timothy; Chapter 6: Verse 10-11)

^{10} For the love of money is a root of all kinds of evil. Some people, eager for money, have wandered from the faith and pierced themselves with many griefs. ^{11} But you, man of God, flee from all this, and pursue righteousness, godliness, faith, love, endurance and gentleness.

（提摩太前書；6章，10-11節）

^{10} 貪財是萬惡之根。有人貪戀錢財，就被引誘離了真道，用許多愁苦把自己刺透了。^{11} 但你這屬神的人要逃避這些事，追求公義、敬虔、信心、愛心、忍耐、溫柔。

Vocabulary

root [rut] n. 根
eager [ˋigɚ] adj. 渴望的
faith [feθ] n. 信仰
grief [grif] n. 悲痛
evil [ˋivəl] n. 邪惡
wander [ˋwandɚ] v. 離開正道
pierce [pɪrs] v. 刺穿
pursue [pɚˋsu] v. 追求

For the love of money is a root of all kinds of evil. Some people, eager for money, have wandered from the faith and pierced themselves with many griefs. But you, man of God, flee from all this, and pursue righteousness, godliness, faith, love, endurance and gentleness.

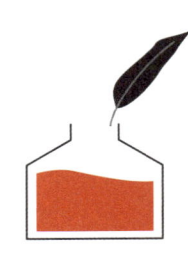

Day 130
有了知識要加節制
Add Self-control to Your Knowledge

(2 Peter; Chapter 1: Verse 5-7)

⁵ For this very reason, make every effort to add to your faith goodness; and to goodness, knowledge; ⁶ and to knowledge, self-control; and to self-control, perseverance; and to perseverance, godliness; ⁷ and to godliness, mutual affection; and to mutual affection, love.

（彼得後書；1章，5-7節）

⁵ 正因這緣故，你們要分外的殷勤；有了信心，又要加上德行；有了德行，又要加上知識；⁶ 有了知識，又要加上節制；有了節制，又要加上忍耐；有了忍耐，又要加上虔敬；⁷ 有了虔敬，又要加上愛弟兄的心；有了愛弟兄的心，又要加上愛眾人的心；

Vocabulary

reason [ˈrizən] n. 理由
add [æd] v. 增加
goodness [ˈgʊdnəs] n. 美德
self-control [ˌsɛlfkənˈtrol] n. 自制
godliness [ˈgɑdlɪnəs] n. 虔誠，敬畏神的心
affection [əˈfɛkʃən] n. 情感

effort [ˈɛfɚt] n. 努力
faith [feθ] n. 信仰
knowledge [ˈnɑlɪdʒ] n. 知識
perseverance [ˌpɝsəˈvɪrəns] n. 堅持不懈
mutual [ˈmjuːtʃuəl] adj. 互相的

For this very reason, make every effort to add to your faith goodness; and to goodness, knowledge; and to knowledge, self-control; and to self-control, perseverance; and to perseverance, godliness; and to godliness, mutual affection; and to mutual affection, love.

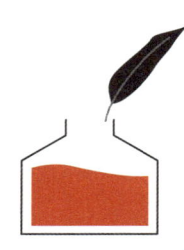

Day 131
享受美食也要節制
Enjoy Delicious Food in Moderation

(Proverbs; Chapter 25: Verse 16-17)

¹⁶ If you find honey, eat just enough— too much of it, and you will vomit. ¹⁷ Seldom set foot in your neighbor's house— too much of you, and they will hate you.

（箴言；25 章，16-17 節）

¹⁶ 你得了蜜嗎？只可吃夠而已，恐怕你過飽就嘔吐出來。¹⁷ 你的腳要少進鄰舍的家，恐怕他厭煩你，恨惡你。

Vocabulary

honey [ˈhʌnɪ] **n.** 蜂蜜
enough [ɪˈnʌf] **adv.** 足夠
seldom [ˈsɛldəm] **adv.** 很少
neighbor [ˈnebɚ] **adj.** 鄰居
hate [het] **v.** 討厭

eat [it] **v.** 吃
vomit [ˈvɑmɪt] **v.** 嘔吐
set foot 去（某處）
house [haʊs] **n.** 房子

If you find honey, eat just enough— too much of it, and you will vomit. Seldom set foot in your neighbor's house— too much of you, and they will hate you.

Day 132

凡事作為不受轄制
Don't Be Mastered by Anything

(1 Corinthians; Chapter 6: Verse 12)

¹² "I have the right to do anything," you say—but not everything is beneficial. "I have the right to do anything"—but I will not be mastered by anything.

（哥林多前書；6章，12節）

¹² 凡事我都可行，但不都有益處。凡事我都可行，但無論哪一件，我總不受它的轄制。

Vocabulary

right [raɪt] **n.** 權利

master [ˋmæstɚ] **v.** 制伏；控制

beneficial [ˌbɛnɪˋfɪʃəl] **adj.** 有益的

everything [ˋɛvrɪθɪŋ] **pron.** 一切

"I have the right to do anything," you say—but not everything is beneficial. "I have the right to do anything"—but I will not be mastered by anything.

Day 133

謹言慎行以免犯罪
Watch My Ways and Keep My Tongue from Sin

(Psalm 39: Verse 1)

¹ I said, "I will watch my ways and keep my tongue from sin; I will put a muzzle on my mouth while in the presence of the wicked."

（詩篇；39 篇，1 節）

¹ 我曾說：我要謹慎我的言行，免得我舌頭犯罪；惡人在我面前的時候，我要用嚼環勒住我的口。

Vocabulary

watch [wɑtʃ] v. 觀看，注意
keep [kip] v. 保持
sin [sɪn] n. 罪
mouth [maʊθ] n. 嘴
wicked [ˈwɪkɪd] adj. 邪惡的

way [we] n. 方式
tongue [tʌŋ] n. 舌頭
muzzle [ˈmʌzl] n. 口套
presence [ˈprɛzəns] n. 存在，出現

I said, "I will watch my ways and keep my tongue from sin; I will put a muzzle on my mouth while in the presence of the wicked."

Day 134

為神管家凡事節制
Be Self-controlled as an Overseer of God's Household

(Titus; Chapter 1: Verse 7-8)

7 Since an overseer manages God's household, he must be blameless—not overbearing, not quick-tempered, not given to drunkenness, not violent, not pursuing dishonest gain. **8** Rather, he must be hospitable, one who loves what is good, who is self-controlled, upright, holy and disciplined.

(提多書；1章，7-8節)

7 監督既是神的管家，必須無可指責，不任性，不暴躁，不因酒滋事，不打人，不貪無義之財。**8** 樂意接待遠人，好善，莊重，公平，聖潔自持。

Vocabulary

overseer [ˈovɚˌsɪr] **n.** 監督者
household [ˈhaʊsˌhold] **n.** 家庭
overbearing [ˌovɚˈbɛrɪŋ] **adj.** 專橫的；傲慢的
drunkenness [ˈdrʌŋkənnɪs] **n.** 酗酒
dishonest [dɪsˈɑnɪst] **adj.** 不誠實的

manage [ˈmænɪdʒ] **v.** 管理
blameless [ˈblemləs] **adj.** 無可指責的
quick-tempered 脾氣急躁的
violent [ˈvaɪələnt] **adj.** 暴力的
hospitable [hɑˈspɪtəbl] **adj.** 好客的

Since an overseer manages God's household, he must be blameless—not overbearing, not quick-tempered, not given to drunkenness, not violent, not pursuing dishonest gain. Rather, he must be hospitable, one who loves what is good, who is self-controlled, upright, holy and disciplined.

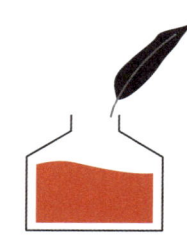

Day 135

勸老年人要有節制
Teach the Older Men to Be Self-controlled

(Titus; Chapter 2: Verse 2-3)

² Teach the older men to be temperate, worthy of respect, self-controlled, and sound in faith, in love and in endurance. ³ Likewise, teach the older women to be reverent in the way they live, not to be slanderers or addicted to much wine, but to teach what is good.

（提多書；2章，2-3節）

² 勸老年人要有節制、端莊、自守，在信心、愛心、忍耐上都要純全無疵。³ 又勸老年婦人，舉止行動要恭敬，不說讒言，不給酒作奴僕，用善道教訓人，

Vocabulary

teach [titʃ] v. 教導
temperate [ˈtɛmpərət] adj. 有節制的
respect [rɪˈspɛkt] n. 尊重
sound [saʊnd] adj. 健全的
endurance [ɪnˈdʊrəns] n. 忍耐
slanderer [ˈslændərɚ] n. 誹謗者

older [ˈoldɚ] adj. 年長的
worthy [ˈwɝðɪ] adj. 值得的
self-controlled [ˌsɛlfkənˈtrold] adj. 自制的
faith [feθ] n. 信心
reverent [ˈrɛvərənt] adj. 恭敬的
addicted [əˈdɪktɪd] adj. 上癮的

Teach the older men to be temperate, worthy of respect, self-controlled, and sound in faith, in love and in endurance. Likewise, teach the older women to be reverent in the way they live, not to be slanderers or addicted to much wine, but to teach what is good.

台灣廣廈 國際出版集團
Taiwan Mansion International Group

國家圖書館出版品預行編目（CIP）資料

祝福人生的英文聖經抄寫奇蹟：聖靈的果實 / 林大煜（聖句摘錄人員）. -- 初版. -- 新北市：國際學村出版社, 2025.04
　　面；　公分
ISBN 978-986-454-415-8（平裝）
1.CST: 聖經　2.CST: 英語　3.CST: 讀本

805.18　　　　　　　　　　　　　　　　　114002219

國際學村

祝福人生的英文聖經抄寫奇蹟-聖靈的果實

聖句摘錄人員／林大煜	編輯中心編輯長／伍峻宏・編輯／古竣元 封面設計／陳沛涓・內頁排版／菩薩蠻數位文化有限公司 製版・印刷・裝訂／東豪・弼聖・秉成

行企研發中心總監／陳冠蒨　　　線上學習中心總監／陳冠蒨
媒體公關組／陳柔彣　　　　　　企製開發組／張哲剛
綜合業務組／何欣穎

發　行　人／江媛珍
法律顧問／第一國際法律事務所 余淑杏律師・北辰著作權事務所 蕭雄淋律師
出　　版／國際學村
發　　行／台灣廣廈有聲圖書有限公司
　　　　　地址：新北市235中和區中山路二段359巷7號2樓
　　　　　電話：（886）2-2225-5777・傳真：（886）2-2225-8052
讀者服務信箱／cs@booknews.com.tw

代理印務・全球總經銷／知遠文化事業有限公司
　　　　　地址：新北市222深坑區北深路三段155巷25號5樓
　　　　　電話：（886）2-2664-8800・傳真：（886）2-2664-8801
郵政劃撥／劃撥帳號：18836722
　　　　　劃撥戶名：知遠文化事業有限公司（※單次購書金額未達1000元，請另付70元郵資。）

■出版日期：2025年04月　　　ISBN：978-986-454-415-8
　　　　　　　　　　　　　　版權所有，未經同意不得重製、轉載、翻印。

Complete Copyright © 2025 by Taiwan Mansion Publishing Co., Ltd.
All rights reserved.